Dear Reader,

Did you ever watch cartoons where one of the characters is painting the floor and he winds up painting himself into a corner with no way out? Eventually, the character paints a door on the wall and is able to get out. Well, coming up with a unique mystery is kind of like the same thing. In wanting to make the story unusual, I found that I had painted myself into a corner and I really wasn't sure how to get out of it.

In this story, a venerable old hotel is finally sold to make way for more residential developments. A construction company wins the bid and brings in their crew. However, as the wrecking ball brings down the hotel's walls, bodies start turning up. How the bodies got into the walls without anyone noticing was the corner I had painted myself into.

Solving the case is what homicide detective Brianna Cavanaugh O'Bannon and major crimes detective Jackson Muldare are up against. As the story progresses, Jackson finds he has a far better chance of solving the forty-five-year-old cold case than getting Brianna to stay out of his life. Read this to find out who wins—and who killed all those people.

As always, I thank you very much for taking the time to read one of my books, and from the bottom of my heart, I wish you someone to love who loves you back.

All the best,

Marie Ferrarella

CAVANAUGH VANGUARD

Marie Ferrarella

HARLEQUIN® ROMANTIC SUSPENSE

Recycling programs
for this product may
not exist in your area.

ISBN-13: 978-1-335-45635-9

Cavanaugh Vanguard

Copyright © 2018 by Marie Rydzynski-Ferrarella

HARLEQUIN®
www.Harlequin.com

Printed in U.S.A.

USA TODAY bestselling and RITA® Award–winning author **Marie Ferrarella** has written more than two hundred and fifty books for Harlequin, some under the name Marie Nicole. Her romances are beloved by fans worldwide. Visit her website, marieferrarella.com.

Visit the Author Profile page at Harlequin.com for more titles.

To
Sherry & Rick
Congratulations!
Fifty Down,
Fifty To Go
The First One Hundred Years
Are The Hardest,
After That, It's A Piece Of Cake!

Prologue

"Hey, boss man, I think you're going to want to see this!"

Javier Hernandez, head foreman of Preston, Butler & Cowan Construction, which had, after an intense bidding war, wound up submitting the winning bid to tear down the Old Aurora Hotel, the city of Aurora's oldest landmark still in existence, emerged out of the building in a dead run. The tall, sinewy foreman was searching for the company's owner.

Warren Preston was just about to get into his silver-gray 4x4. The freshly waxed, newly purchased truck had been Preston's gift to himself after landing the contract.

It was Preston's habit to visit a site on the first day that work was to begin. He'd done it with his very first project, and over the years what had begun as a display of involvement for his men had turned into a superstition, one that he had never taken lightly or ignored. No matter how busy he was, Preston made a point to show up on that crucial first day and remain for at least a few hours. After day one, his visits were sporadic at best—unless there was a problem.

Turning away now from his new pride and joy, he left the door of his truck open as he looked at the foreman rushing toward him.

Judging by the expression on Javier's face, there was definitely a problem.

How could there be a problem? Preston wondered. The workday was barely a couple of hours old.

This morning the demolition ball had mightily swung into the rear wall of what had once been an elegant structure. When the Old Aurora Hotel had first gone up, it had been the first of its kind, not just in the newly formed town, but in the county as well. George Aurora was said to have worked on the building himself.

A great many people in and around Aurora had fought the historic hotel's demise, wanting to preserve the sprawling three-story structure for a host of reasons.

But, as was often the case, money trumped history and sentiment. The land on which the old, boarded-up hotel stood was worth a fortune. Aurora had grown from a small, three-traffic-light town surrounded by farmland to a thriving, ever-expanding city. A city where, it seemed, everyone wanted to live.

Land was at a premium, and an old hotel that was no longer of any use became a casualty of that siren song. Decisions were made, money changed hands and the hotel was to be demolished to make way for a brand-new, state-of-the-art residential development.

After a run of bad luck and investments that hadn't panned out, Warren Preston was counting on this development to put his construction company back on the map—and in the running for more construction bids farther down south.

That was why everything had to go smoothly with this job.

"Javi, I'm late for a meeting. Can't this wait?" Preston asked impatiently. With one foot still in his truck, Preston was ready to take off the second his foreman backed off.

"I don't think so, sir," Javier answered.

The foreman's stance and his body language made clear that he was waiting to reenter the building he'd just vacated—but only with his boss in tow.

"What's with the long face, Javi?" Preston asked, resigned to the fact that he would be late for his meeting. Leaving his vehicle, Preston closed the door. "Buck up—this is the first day of a brand-new project. Everything's still fresh and new. Hell, man, you look like somebody died."

"That's just it, boss," Javier answered solemnly. "I think somebody did."

Bushy eyebrows drew together above small brown eyes, looking for all the world like two caterpillars awkwardly attempting to rise up as Preston glared at the man who had worked for him for over fifteen years.

"What the hell are you talking about, Hernandez?" he demanded. "Who died?"

Rather than answer, Javier was beckoning for his boss to follow him.

Taller than Preston and leaner than his boss by half his weight, Javier had a lengthy stride that put more and more distance between his boss and him. Clearly agitated, Javier seemed to be restraining himself from breaking into a run.

Hernandez insisted, "You have to see this for yourself."

"See what?" Preston snapped, trying to catch up with the younger man. "I don't have time for guessing games, Hernandez," he warned.

"It's not a game, boss," the foreman assured Preston. "I only wish it was."

He brought the construction company owner into the rear of the hotel that had been designed to emulate an elegant Southern mansion.

The dining room had been considered exceptionally stylish and upscale in its day, but time and the elements that had seeped into the structure had not been kind. The expensive wallpaper that had graced the walls had long since begun peeling.

Standing in the doorway, Preston fisted his hands at his ample waist as he irritably scanned the area. Daylight was coming in through the hole where the wrecking ball had made first contact.

"Okay, so what's this big emergency?" Preston demanded.

"Right there, sir."

Javier pointed to the reason he had urgently called for both workers and machinery to come to an absolute grinding halt. To the right of where the wrecking ball had left its first startling imprint, knocking down part of a wall, what looked like a skeletal hand reached up out of the gaping hole.

Chapter 1

Major crimes detective Jackson Muldare had just exited the southbound 5 freeway when he felt the inside pocket of his sports jacket vibrating.

Again.

He didn't need to pull his cell phone out to know who was calling. It was either his superior, Lieutenant Jonathan Cohen, or the lead homicide detective he was going to be working with at the latest crime scene. Either one of them undoubtedly had the same question for him: Why wasn't he there already?

There was a simple answer for that, but not one he was willing to go into right now.

Just as he was leaving his apartment, he'd got

the call to head out to the Old Aurora Hotel. Although he'd said he'd be there, his first destination of the morning wasn't the site of the old hotel, or even the police precinct. Instead, he'd headed to the Safe Haven Rehab Center. Not because he wanted to but because he had to.

A police detective's salary—at least an honest one's—only stretched so far, and he had already paid the monthly fee for his father's room at Happy Pines, the board and care facility where his father had been living these last three years. Jackson was consequently late with his payment to Safe Haven, the rehab center where Jimmy was currently staying.

He made it to the center with his check by the skin of his teeth. Though sympathetic, Alice Harris, the administrator who was in charge of the center's business office, had told him that if he hadn't come through with the payment by the end of this business day, Jackson's younger brother would have found himself back out on the street.

Jackson had paid the woman, telling her solemnly that it wouldn't happen again. He'd left quickly before his temper got the better of him and he said something he couldn't take back. He was well aware that Ms. Harris and the center held all the cards, forcing him to keep his thoughts to himself. He was doing his best, but the money he earned only stretched so far, and on occasion, he came up short.

There were times, Jackson thought as he turned

on the siren and flashing lights that allowed him to cut through the city's traffic, when he found himself almost regretting that he'd turned his back on a life of crime.

Almost.

In his teens, the guys he hung around with in his old Oakland neighborhood had all dropped out of school and declared that staying on the straight and narrow was only for gutless losers. The thinking back then was that guys with guts could find all sorts of ways of gaming the system, lining their pockets with money and achieving the good life at the expense of others.

More than a few of his so-called friends ridiculed him for his choice to actually work for the money he brought home. But crime had never been an option for him. Jackson had people to take care of.

His mother had walked out on the family when he was ten, and his father, Ethan, although a kind-hearted, loving man, had also been a functioning alcoholic who anesthetized his sense of failure with any bottle of alcohol he could get his hands on. He wasn't choosy. Anything would do. Eventually, Ethan Muldare ceased functioning and just devoted himself exclusively to drinking.

The burden of providing for his family and keeping them together had fallen to Jackson by the time he turned fifteen.

Fourteen years later, he was still shouldering that burden. For the last three years he'd been paying for his father's tiny room at the board and care residential facility. All those years of drinking had taken their toll on his father's health as well as on the man's mental faculties.

And because their mother had taken off and their father had turned to alcohol for solace, his younger brother, Jimmy, had sought relief in drugs by the time he was thirteen.

There were days when Jackson found it hard to keep it all together and keep going. Those were the days when he seriously entertained the idea of getting in his car and just driving as far away from his life as he possibly could.

But that was just the problem. No matter where he went, he always took himself and his sense of responsibility with him.

What that meant was that he had no choice but to do what he did. Someone had to pay the bills and to set an example, such as it was, for Jimmy. On good days Jackson still nursed the minuscule hope that eventually Jimmy would come around and realize that numbing his mind and his soul with drugs was just not the answer.

If anything, it was a death sentence.

Jackson supposed, at bottom, there was just the tiniest bit of an optimist within him.

He felt his phone vibrating again.

Jackson resisted the temptation of pulling it out and shouting that he was on his way. Yelling at Lt. Cohen would most likely get him suspended—or fired. Yelling at whoever he was being paired up with would, at the very least, start him off on the wrong foot, and he already had more than enough to deal with on the home front.

Jimmy had been hostile during the three minutes he'd had to talk to him, and when he'd swung by Happy Pines his father hadn't recognized him. That was happening more and more often these days. Jackson just wasn't in the frame of mind to make nice to whoever was on the phone, so he let it continue to vibrate and drove faster.

He was almost there anyway.

"You know, if I read about this kind of thing online or in the paper, I would have said that someone made it up," homicide detective Brianna Cavanaugh O'Bannon said, shaking her head as she took in the chaotic scene around her.

"Oh, but you can't make this kind of stuff up," Sean Cavanaugh commented.

The head of the Crime Scene Investigative day team frowned as, like his niece, he slowly regarded the partially demolished hotel.

"No, I guess not," Brianna agreed.

This was, she thought, a case of fact being stranger than fiction. With slow, deliberate movements, she picked her way through the debris, both newly created and old. She was careful not to disturb anything. At this point, it was still difficult sorting out what was part of the crime scene and what was just run-of-the-mill, everyday rubble.

Looking back over her shoulder, Brianna saw the chief of detectives entering the room. It was obvious to her that the tall, distinguished-looking man was temporarily transported back through time as he recalled, "You know, I can remember Aurora High holding their senior prom here the year I graduated."

"What are you doing here?" Sean asked, no doubt surprised to see his younger brother. "The chief of detectives doesn't usually come out to a crime scene."

"He does if the scene is in the Old Aurora Hotel," Brian Cavanaugh replied. Setting his memories aside, he became practical. "How many bodies?" he asked.

"Six—and counting," Brianna answered.

Brian Cavanaugh didn't frown often, but he did now. "Damn," he murmured.

"That would be the word I'd use," Sean agreed. "I've got a feeling that we're going to need more medical examiners on the job by the time we finish."

"Who do we have on it right now?" Brian asked.

Sean nodded toward his left. The ME and her assistant were closing up a body bag and placing the occupant on a gurney.

"Malloy's wife, Kristin," Sean answered.

Brian's smile was grim. "This is turning out to be a regular family affair," he commented, glancing toward the young woman. "Put the word out," he told his brother. "We need every available ME reporting to the morgue. I need these bodies identified yesterday," Brian instructed.

Sean had his cell phone in his hand. "Already on it," he responded.

"Keep me apprised," Brian said, leaving. It was unclear if he was addressing Sean or Brianna.

Brianna slowly scanned the area again, even though she had been here for more than half an hour. She and Francisco Del Campo, another homicide detective, had been the first to answer the frantic call that had come in from a patrol officer.

The latter had been the first responder on the scene. Fresh out of the academy, Officer Hal Jacobs had contaminated the crime scene by throwing up after viewing the first decomposing body. When Brianna arrived, she had hustled Jacobs out and had someone get the pale officer a glass of water as more bodies were being discovered.

A noise coming from behind her had Brianna whirling around, one hand on her weapon, ready for anything.

Coming forward, Jackson raised his hands. "If you don't want me here, all you have to do is say so," he told Brianna.

Brianna dropped her hand to her side. Although they were in different divisions, she and Jackson had previously worked together on a couple of cases. As far as partners went, he was intelligent and driven.

He just wasn't much of a conversationalist, but according to the job description, that wasn't a prerequisite.

"Nice of you to join the party, Detective Muldare," she said.

Rather than explain why he'd arrived late, Jackson merely said, "I got held up in traffic. What are we looking at?"

"The stuff nightmares are made of," she told him. "You ever been here before?"

"You mean to the hotel?" he asked. When she nodded, he told her, "I didn't grow up in Aurora. And I'm guessing the place would have been a little out of my price range if I *had* grown up here."

Brianna looked around, trying to envision the hotel the way it used to be in what she'd heard referred to as its "glory days." It made her sad to see the way time had ravaged it.

"It was a hell of a showplace in its time. I saw pictures in a magazine once," she explained. "Aurora was celebrating its fortieth anniversary of being incorporated as a city and the magazine article was a then-and-now kind of retrospective. I really doubt that anyone would have ever suspected that this highly regarded showplace was where someone was hiding bodies."

"Hiding bodies?" Jackson echoed.

Brianna nodded, repeating what she'd heard from the nauseated first responder. "They were in the walls," she told him. "The wrecking ball uncovered them."

The macabre revelation had Jackson staring at her in disbelief. "You're kidding."

Brianna turned toward the major crimes detective. She wasn't quite sure what to make of his reaction. The tall, dark-haired man seemed woefully uninformed about the nature of the crime scene he had entered. "Didn't anyone tell you?"

"Cohen just said to get my butt out here," Jackson answered. "Look, I'm with major crimes," he pointed out even though he knew that she knew that. "And while this is all pretty gruesome, I don't know what I'm supposed to be doing here." He looked at Brianna. "Way I see it, since you're with homicide, this case is right up your alley."

"You've been with the police department for how long now?" she asked him, her voice almost mild and deceptively conversational.

He didn't see what that had to do with anything, but he answered her. "Going on six years now."

"Six years," she repeated, as if she was rolling the information over in her head. "Don't take much of an interest in the city's history, do you?"

Jackson looked at the woman. Like so many other members of the police department he had run into, she was part of the Cavanaugh family, a legend throughout the precinct. Cavanaughs, he'd found, set the bar high, each and every one of them.

"Not particularly," he answered. "Why?"

"Well, if you did know a little of the city's history," she told him, "you'd know that initially this was all farmland that belonged to one family. The Aurora family."

"All right," he allowed, still waiting to hear where she was going with all this.

Out of the corner of her eye, Brianna saw the ME, Kristin Alberghetti-Cavanaugh, wheeling another one of the newly unearthed victims out of the hotel. She stepped to one side, never missing a beat of the story she was telling Jackson.

"George Aurora was the original patriarch of the family. He started taking the money the family made selling their crops and investing it. The investments were solid, so he decided to use some of the profits to build a small town, which he named after himself.

"Everything in and around Aurora belonged to the Aurora family. Including the Aurora Hotel," she pointed out, adding, "which, it turns out, Winston Aurora, George's oldest grandson, recently sold to the city so that Aurora could continue to expand."

"Winston's the one who throws all those fundraisers, raising money to build that new children's hospital and new schools for the city, right?" Jackson said, recalling things that he'd heard.

"One and the same," Brianna confirmed. "No one wants to risk getting on the wrong side of the man or his two brothers if they don't have to, so I'm told that major crimes was called in to treat this whole thing—and the Aurora family—with kid gloves."

The strained smile on her face as she concluded told Jackson just what she thought of that idea, seeing as how he was the one the major crimes lieutenant had chosen to represent the division.

Jackson read between the lines. "Are you saying you think Mr. Fund-Raiser is responsible for the dead bodies?"

"I'm saying we're supposed to look at everyone else first before we even so much as *think* of pointing a finger at him or anyone else in his family. Having major crimes join homicide in the investigation is supposed to be the police department's way of being thorough," Brianna told him. "That means crossing every single *t* and dotting every single *i*. And if I recall correctly from the last couple of times you and I worked together, you are not exactly known as Mr. Diplomacy, so maybe I should be the one to talk to the Auroras."

"Are we going to be questioning the Auroras first?" Jackson asked.

"No, not in the way you mean," Brianna answered, thinking he was referring to interrogating the family. "We're just going to inform them of what the construction crew discovered when they started knocking down the walls."

Brianna paused for a moment. She'd been told more than once that she had a habit of taking over and leaping into the heart of things before others around her had a chance to digest what was happening. Since she and Muldare were going to be working together on this, she knew she had to do her best not to come on as strong as she had a tendency to. "Unless you have a different idea on the matter," she added tactfully.

Jackson lifted his wide shoulders then let them fall again in a careless shrug. "My only thought is that maybe we should hold off talking to Mr. Fund-Raiser or anyone in his family until we have a final body count."

She supposed that Jackson did have a point, but there was a problem with this idea. She glanced over toward where Sean and his team were working.

"I'm not sure how long that would take," she said honestly. "The building only has three stories, but it's unusually wide. Consequently, there are a lot of walls to take into account."

"You really think there are more bodies in them?" Jackson questioned.

She wouldn't have thought that there were any bodies in the walls, but that certainly hadn't turned out to be the case.

"You think there aren't?" Brianna countered.

"Sounds a little unbelievable, don't you think?" Jackson asked, getting out of the way as another gurney with a body bag was being wheeled out.

"I think finding a single body buried inside a hotel wall is unbelievable, but according to what

I've been told, they've uncovered six," Brianna an-swered.

"Seven," Sean called out.

Brianna and Jackson both turned in the man's direction.

"Seven?" Brianna asked, stunned.

Sean nodded. "Destiny just told me that the team pulled out another body," he replied, referring to his top CSI investigator, his son Logan's wife.

Brianna closed her eyes for a moment, trying to absorb the information and ignore the effect the discovery was having on her stomach.

What kind of a monster had they just stumbled across? And, more important, was that monster still walking among them, or was this the work of someone who had vanished?

Best-case scenario was that the killer was dead. But what if the killer wasn't dead and hadn't van-ished? What if the killer had just moved his desire to kill to another location?

"You okay?" Jackson asked. He saw his new partner shiver. It definitely wasn't cold in the room, despite the fact that there was one wall missing.

"I will be," Brianna answered with zeal. "Once we find the SOB responsible for this."

Chapter 2

Jackson silently agreed with the detective he had been temporarily partnered with. "Then I guess we'd better get started," he told Brianna.

Nodding, she turned toward Francisco Del Campo. Transferred to homicide a little over six months ago, the personable detective was still learning the ropes and had no problem taking orders from a woman.

"What would you like me to do?" Del Campo asked.

"Find out exactly when the hotel closed its doors and see if you can get your hands on the hotel's guest ledger up to that point," Brianna said. She felt that at least it was a start.

Del Campo furrowed his brow. "How far back do you want to go?"

"Since we don't know how many bodies are in the walls and how long they've been there, why don't you see how far back you can go," Jackson told the younger man.

Rather than getting right on it, Del Campo shifted his eyes toward Brianna, waiting for her confirmation. He knew Brianna. He didn't know Jackson.

She nodded. "What he said," she told Del Campo, hoping that, at least for the time being, they could all work harmoniously. "I also want you to get all the construction workers' names. We'll need to question them if they saw anything unusual. Right now, we don't know where those bodies came from or who put them there."

"You got it." Del Campo was already on his way out of the partially gutted dining room.

The moment Del Campo left, Jackson turned toward the woman on his left. "You know, this is going to go a lot easier if I don't need your stamp of approval every time I say something."

Brianna smiled at the major crimes detective. "I was just thinking the same thing."

Jackson pressed his lips together and kept his comment to himself.

They made their way out of the hotel, weaving around various members of the police department and crime scene investigators. Once outside, Brianna paused for a moment and took a deep breath.

The air smelled sweeter away from the combined odors of death and dust. Out of the corner of her eye, she caught Jackson looking at her. "You want to drive?" she asked as she started to walk again.

"You don't want to arm wrestle for it?" he asked, feigning surprise.

"Normally I'd consider it," she deadpanned. "But Del Campo and I came here together, and he's going to need a way to get back to the precinct."

"So I get to do the honors by default, is that it?" Jackson guessed.

She'd started walking toward where she assumed Jackson had left his unmarked vehicle but she stopped now. The man definitely had a chip on his shoulder. She didn't remember him being this way the last time they'd worked together.

"Look, if you're going to want to debate every single move, this case is going to go a lot slower than either one of us—or the chief of Ds—is going to be happy about," she told him. And then, getting into the car, she got down to the real question. "Do you have a problem working with me this time, Muldare?"

She wasn't the one responsible for his mood. That had been set in motion before he'd got the call to come out here. Jackson knew he shouldn't be taking it out on her or subjecting her to any fallout.

"No," Jackson answered. And then he tagged on a word he hoped would cover the situation. "Sorry."

"Don't be sorry," Brianna said. "Just don't do it." And then she got down to the business at hand. "If we're going to be delivering bad news to one of Aurora's three leading citizens, we need to present a united front. Otherwise Winston Aurora might get the idea we're accusing him of being responsible for these bodies."

"What if he is?" Jackson asked.

That was a giant leap, but it still could be true, she thought.

"We'll cross that bridge when we come to it—and brace ourselves for all hell breaking loose just for asking." She glanced at him as she buckled up. "What are your thoughts on this?"

Jackson shrugged, buckling up himself. "Don't have any."

"None?" she questioned incredulously. That didn't seem possible—or logical.

"Nope," he said as casually as if he was deciding how many eggs he wanted for breakfast. "That might taint my view of the case and interfere with the way I investigate it."

Listening to him, Brianna could only shake her head. "You are a strange bird, Jackson Muldare."

He laughed drily. "So I've been told."

"Why aren't you starting the car?" she asked.

"Because you haven't told me where we'll find

this guy," Jackson answered. "Where do you want to go?"

She'd forgotten about that. "We'll start at Winston Aurora's home. If he's attending some board meeting or some other business-related activity, his wife or someone at the house should be able to tell us where he is." She looked at Jackson expectantly. "You do know where Winston Aurora lives, right?"

Jackson didn't answer her. Instead, he started up the white sedan and pulled out of the parking lot.

The lot was still crowded with vehicles belonging to the officers who had responded to the call, as well as those of the construction workers who had been told to stop work on the demolition immediately. Del Campo was still taking down the latter group's names, Brianna noted, seeing the detective talking to a group of hard hats.

"Oh damn," Brianna said.

"Is that a general, all-inclusive 'oh damn,' or are you referring to something specific?" Jackson asked, keeping his eyes on the road.

Brianna twisted around in her seat, peering out the rear window. There was a news van pulling up toward the cluster of police cars.

"That's a 'make sure that news van doesn't suddenly decide to follow you' oh damn," she answered. She twisted forward again. "The last thing we need or want is someone from the Fourth Estate thinking we're going to be talking to Winston Aurora or anyone in his family."

"But we are," Jackson answered matter-of-factly.

She wondered if he was putting her on or if he just viewed situations in a linear fashion. For the sake of argument, she explained it to him.

"We want to keep a lid on this and control the story for as long as we can until we know if there *is* a story involving the Auroras."

"We already know there are bodies," Jackson pointed out.

"Yes, but what we don't know is if the Auroras' connection ends with the fact that the hotel was built by their grandfather and bears their name— or if one of them is more involved than that," she told Jackson. "If the media gets hold of this before we're ready, there'll be so much speculation going on, we won't be able to do our jobs properly."

Jackson said nothing.

She found it annoying and felt as if she was talking to herself.

Suddenly, the detective deviated from the road he was on. The next moment he was pulling his vehicle into a drive-through lane threading around a fast-food restaurant called Sloppy Joes.

"What are you doing?" Brianna demanded.

Jackson spared her a quick glance before inching the car forward. They were behind a Hummer 3 that was just barely keeping between the lines.

"Making sure that news van doesn't think we're onto something and follow us—haven't you been paying attention to what you just said?" he asked innocently.

For a split second, she wanted to punch him, but she refrained, thinking she'd do more damage to her fist than to his really muscular shoulder.

Instead, Brianna laughed. "I forgot." As she recalled, Muldare had an unorthodox method of operation. "You take some getting used to."

Jackson made no comment on her observation. "Since we're here, you want to get something?"

Food was the last thing on her mind. Brianna twisted around in her seat again. There was no sign of the news van. It hadn't followed them after all.

Sitting forward again, she told Jackson, "Coffee, black."

His expression remained stoic. "That stuff'll rot out your gut," he told her.

Unfazed by the image that created, Brianna said, "Haven't you heard? Coffee is supposed to help keep dementia at bay."

"That's this week's theory," he said, unimpressed. "Next week they'll rescind that theory and replace it with something else."

Brianna shrugged. "Doesn't matter. I like coffee. It keeps me going."

"Those are called nerves," he told her as he placed the order—coffee for her, nothing for him—then pulled to the next window.

"Anyone ever tell you that you can be a real

downer?" Brianna asked as she took out a five-dollar bill to hand him.

Eyes forward, Jackson waved away her money. "Yeah, you," he answered. "The last time we worked together, as I recall."

"Well, I guess nothing's changed," she told him. She waited as Jackson paid the woman at the drive-through window for the coffee and then handed the covered container to her.

"Not a real fan of change," Jackson answered matter-of-factly as he drove away from the fast-food restaurant.

She could believe that, Brianna thought, but she kept that to herself.

Holding the container in both hands, Brianna looked around in all directions. There was no sign of the news van anywhere. "Looks like you lost them."

"That was the intention," he answered matter-of-factly.

Brianna took a long sip of her coffee, then put the lid back on. "Still the sparkling conversationalist, I see."

Jackson glanced in her direction, then looked forward again. "Sparkling conversation was not a prerequisite for graduating from the academy."

Brianna studied his profile for a long moment. "Maybe it should have been," she said. "By the way, thanks for the coffee." She raised the container to her lips again.

"Don't mention it," Jackson told her. "I'm serious," he added before she could respond in any way. "Don't mention it."

Brianna sighed. This was going to be a really long, long investigation.

The road leading to Winston Aurora's forty-thousand-square-foot mansion—by no stretch of the imagination could the structure be referred to as a mere house—was scenic, long and winding. Exceedingly winding.

"Doesn't this road ever end?" Jackson muttered under his breath.

"Doesn't feel that way, does it?" Brianna agreed. "Maybe they want you to feel like you got lost so you'll just finally give up and turn around," she guessed. "But if that is the thinking on their part, they forgot to take one important thing into account."

Silence hung between them until Jackson finally asked, "And that is…?"

She offered him a self-satisfied smile. "We don't give up."

"We?" he deliberately questioned. He wasn't accustomed to "we." For as long as he could remember, he'd thought of himself as a loner, not as someone who was part of something for more than a few moments at a time.

"The police department," Brianna told him with a touch of impatience in her voice. Was he deliberately making things difficult? "Work with me here, Muldare."

"Doing my best," Jackson replied in a voice that couldn't have sounded more disinterested if he'd intentionally tried.

She gave him a penetrating look that would have made any other man squirm. "No, you're not," Brianna countered.

Without a word in his own defense, Jackson spared her a quick glance before looking back at the road.

The path to the mansion was growing progressively narrower. Jackson half expected to see mountain goats dotting the area any second now. He hadn't thought that any part of Aurora was still this pastoral looking.

"Is this where I'm supposed to argue with you?" he asked. "Because if it is, you're going to have to let me in on the game plan, O'Bannon. I'm not much on picking up subtle cues."

That was for sure, Brianna thought. Out loud she said, "The plan is for you to get your head back in the game and pay attention."

A dark expression came over his face. "I thought that was what I was doing."

She shifted in her seat. The hell it was. She only had half his attention, if that much. As far as Brianna could see, there was only one explanation for something like that.

"You don't want to be here, do you?" she asked point-blank.

"Going to talk to some rich guy who thinks because he has enough money to buy a city, that means he's above the rules?" Jackson guessed. "No, not particularly."

"Okay," Brianna allowed. "Then what would you rather be doing?"

That was easy enough to answer. "Identifying the victims. Finding out how they became victims and then tracking down the person who *made* them victims."

Jackson braced himself for an argument. He knew that his mode of operation and his view on things were never the kind to win him popularity contests. But he wasn't in this for popularity. He was here to act on behalf of the victims. To take their side and, whenever possible, to avenge their deaths.

He was surprised when O'Bannon didn't attempt to take him apart.

"All very good goals," Brianna told him, and she genuinely seemed to mean it. "But in order to reach any of those goals, we have to start at the beginning, and the beginning, in this case, is to notify the man who was the last owner of the property of exactly what was found on his property. Who knows? He might say something that will point us in the right direction to find the killer or killers."

Although he appreciated that she didn't attempt

to belittle his viewpoint, he couldn't bring himself to agree with what she'd just said.

He laughed harshly. "You really believe that?"

Brianna regrouped. She did her best not to take offense. That would be petty, and she'd been taught to rise above pettiness. Especially when the stakes were high, as they were here.

"I believe in a lot of things you probably don't," she answered.

"Well, it probably doesn't matter what you believe, because I don't think we're ever going to get to this guy's house," Jackson retorted. The road continued to wind and weave before him like a serpentine river, irritating him no end.

"Oh ye of little faith," Brianna scoffed, irritating him even more. "Look," she said, pointing in the distance. "There. Straight ahead," she told Jackson, then amended, "Well, maybe not so straight, but it's right there, up ahead of us."

One more twist of the road and then he saw it—a mansion that looked as if it had its own zip code.

"I've seen cities that were smaller," Jackson commented under his breath.

Brianna heard him nonetheless. "If I lived here, I'd need a ton of bread crumbs," she said. "Better yet, my own tram."

He thought of the tiny room where his father spent his days and nights. Part of the time, Ethan Muldare was oblivious to not only how small his surroundings were, but *where* they were as well.

"Who needs this much room?" Jackson muttered as he pulled up into the circular driveway.

It was a rhetorical question, but Brianna answered him anyway. "Apparently, Winston Aurora and his family." She had just got out on her side when she saw a young man dressed in what could have passed as valet livery hurrying up to them.

"May I help you?" the man asked in a crisp voice that was far from welcoming.

"We're here to see Mr. Aurora," Brianna said, answering for both of them. "*Winston* Aurora."

The man's eyes washed over them disdainfully. "Do you have an appointment?" His tone indicated that he was certain they didn't.

Jackson took out his badge and ID, holding both aloft. Less than half a beat behind him, Brianna displayed hers.

"We do now," Jackson informed the man he took to be the mansion's head of security.

The man looked at each badge and ID individually. Then, appearing annoyed, he nodded. "Wait right here," he told them curtly.

Turning away, he took out a walkie-talkie and spoke into it in a hushed voice. The unit gave off a loud, piercing squawk, and then a deep voice ordered, "Send them in, Rollins."

Chapter 3

Leaning in toward Jackson, Brianna said in a hushed voice, "Looks like we get to see the wizard after all, Toto."

Jackson frowned. "Toto was a dog."

Brianna merely smiled. "He followed Dorothy wherever she went," she replied, as if, in her opinion, that was enough of a reason for the nickname.

The man who had detained them was back. "Mr. Aurora will see you."

"Yes, Virginia, there is a Santa Claus," Brianna murmured under her breath.

Eyes like highly polished small black marbles narrowed as the head of the estate security looked at her. "Excuse me?"

She was aware that Muldare had taken a single step in front of her, putting himself between her and the powerful-looking head of security.

"Nothing. Please lead the way to Mr. Aurora," Brianna requested, gesturing ahead of the man.

Rollins muttered something unintelligible under his breath as he turned away from them and began to walk toward the mansion.

"That was very noble of you," Brianna whispered to Jackson, looking up at him, a smile flickering over her lips. "Unnecessary, but noble."

"I have no idea what you're talking about," Jackson responded in an unemotional voice. The expression on his face was completely unreadable.

The hell he didn't. Under that dour demeanor, the man was a Boy Scout, Brianna thought. She vaguely remembered that from last time.

"I can take care of myself," Brianna reminded him.

"Never questioned it for a moment," Jackson replied in the same nondescript tone.

How could a man be so annoying and yet so intriguing at the same time, Brianna asked herself. But there was no question in her mind that Jackson was both.

You don't have time for this. You've got bigger things on your agenda right now, remember? Brianna reminded herself as she and Jackson walked behind the estate's head of security and into Winston Aurora's residence.

After a lengthy walk through the first floor, Rollins led them into a room that was twice as large as the dining room in the Old Aurora Hotel had been. It turned out to be one of the mansion's two libraries. There were books lining two of the walls, going from the floor straight up to the vaulted ceiling. One of those walls had a door at its perimeter. Two people, a man and a woman, both in their twenties, were just exiting that way. A third wall was entirely made of tempered glass, allowing afternoon sunlight to bathe the room while effectively keeping the heat at bay.

Seated behind the oversize, highly polished mahogany desk, looking like an emperor presiding over his empire, was Winston Aurora.

Winston Aurora was a man who would have easily taken command of any room he entered. Tanned and slender with distinguished-looking graying hair, he was dressed in a suit that would have easily cost a detective first grade a month's salary—possibly more.

If she hadn't known better, Brianna would have said that the oldest of this generation's three Aurora brothers looked as if he had just stepped out of the pages of *Gentlemen's Quarterly* and into this library.

Rising when he saw them entering, Winston came over to greet them. His smile was amiable and appeared to be completely genuine. He shook both their hands warmly, starting with hers.

"My son and daughter just left," he explained, noting the interest in Brianna's eyes. "Forgive me," Winston said in a deep, resonant voice that was quite pleasing to the ear. "I've lost track. Is it time for the police department's widows and orphans fund-raiser already?" Even as he asked, he was taking a checkbook out of his inside breast pocket.

Brianna put her hand up to stop the man from writing out a check. "We're not here about that, sir, although my uncle said you're always very generous when it comes to making donations to the fund."

"Your uncle," Winston repeated. He raised an eyebrow, asking, "And that would be?"

"Brian Cavanaugh," Brianna responded. "He's the—"

"—chief of detectives, yes, I know," Winston interjected. "I know Brian quite well. Are you here in Brian's place?"

Not answering the multibillionaire's question directly, Brianna bent the truth a little and told Winston, "He said to say hello."

"Ah" was all Winston said, acknowledging what wasn't being said. "Well, if you don't want my donation for any of your worthy causes, how *can* I help you two fine young representatives of the Aurora police department?" Winston asked, looking from one detective to the other.

Brianna glanced over her shoulder. The man who had brought them here was still standing just inside the library threshold like a silent, immovable sentry. While she wasn't afraid of the head of security, the man's presence did make her feel uneasy. "Could we talk alone?"

"Rollins is privy to everything that concerns me. I pay him quite a bit to make sure that he is," Winston said pointedly.

"Then you can tell Rollins all about this after we leave, if you decide he needs to know," Jackson quietly told the older man.

Just a glimmer of displeasure passed over Winston Aurora's smooth, amazingly unlined face. The next moment, the expression disappeared as if it had never existed.

"Very well," Winston agreed. "Rollins, step out, please. I'll let you know if I need you."

Unlike his employer, Rollins made no attempt to mask his displeasure. Scowling, the man withdrew, closing the door behind him.

"Better?" Winston asked Brianna once the door was closed. Whether it was because he thought she was in charge or because he preferred dealing with women was unclear. But his attention was directed to her.

"Our thinking is that you might possibly wind up preferring it this way," Brianna explained.

Winston nodded, making no comment. "Sit, please," he said, indicating the light gray sofa.

Like the desk, the sofa was oversize. It could have accommodated six people without effort.

When the detectives complied, Winston reseated himself behind the desk. For all the world he appeared like a benevolent ruler holding an audience with two of his subjects.

"Now then, I know that Brian's your uncle, but I'm afraid I didn't get your name—or yours," he added, nodding at Jackson.

Brianna automatically reached for her wallet to show the man her credentials. "Detective Brianna Cavanaugh O'Bannon," she answered, pulling out her wallet.

"I'll take you at your word," Winston told her, waving away her wallet, but his brown eyes shifted toward Jackson expectantly.

"Detective Jackson Muldare," Jackson replied.

Winston nodded. "Now that we all know one another, I'll repeat my question. How can I help you?"

"Mr. Aurora—" Brianna began.

"Winston, please," the billionaire corrected her. "'Mr. Aurora' makes me feel ancient." He chuckled. "Please, continue. I didn't mean to interrupt you."

Brianna obliged. Moving forward on her chair, she said, "You recently sold the Old Aurora Hotel."

"Yes, I did," Winston replied, "and if you've come here to tell me that, you could have saved yourself a trip. I'm not quite the doddering old fool yet. I am aware of all of my financial dealings," he assured her with a dry laugh.

"When was the last time you were at the hotel?" Jackson asked, wanting to push this along. O'Bannon might be buying this charming act that Aurora was projecting, but he wasn't sold on it—he thought Aurora seemed to be stalling.

Why the man was stalling wasn't clear yet, but Jackson intended to find that out as well.

"You mean physically?" Winston questioned.

Jackson looked at him, puzzled. "Is there any other way?"

"Well, there's Skyping," Winston answered. "But I closed down the hotel before we could implement that form of communication."

"All right," Jackson said, "when was the last time you were at the hotel in person or in spirit?"

Winston paused, thinking. And then he shrugged. "I'm afraid I really can't remember an exact date. Why? Is it important?" The billionaire turned to direct his question toward Brianna, since she was obviously the friendlier of the two, in the man's estimation.

"What my partner is attempting to do is establish a timeline, sir," Brianna explained.

Winston furrowed his brow. "Why?" Not waiting for either of the two detectives to answer that, he continued, "Is there something wrong, Detectives? Don't tell me that the construction company forgot to get all the right permits."

Wanting to remain on the man's good side, Brianna tactfully answered, "As far as we know, sir, all the permits are in place—"

"Then I'm afraid that I don't understand the reason for all this," the billionaire confessed, waving his hand at both of them. "Just why is it that you're here?"

Brianna couldn't quite decide if what she heard in Aurora's voice was impatience or concern. For now, she let that go.

"When the wrecking ball hit the rear wall, a body was dislodged," she told the man, wanting to proceed slowly.

"Several bodies," Jackson interjected.

Winston looked from one detective to the other, appearing completely caught off guard and speechless. When he finally managed to collect himself, Winston could only echo in hushed disbelief, "Bodies? Whose?"

"That's what we're trying to ascertain, sir," Brianna said.

Winston grew pale right before her eyes. "Do you have any idea who—who killed them?" he asked, his voice almost failing him.

"Another good question," Jackson told him, his tone totally devoid of emotion.

Exasperated and momentarily losing his temper, Winston demanded, "Well, do you have any good *answers*, Detective?"

"Not yet," Brianna answered quickly before Jackson could say something to further irritate Aurora. "But we're doing our best."

Responding to Brianna's soothing voice, Winston seemed to calm down a little. He took in a deep breath, then slowly released it.

"I'm sorry, Detectives. I didn't mean to fly off the handle like that," he apologized. "But I find having bodies uncovered on my former property very upsetting and deeply disturbing."

"We completely understand, Mr. Aurora—" Brianna began.

An almost shy smile quirked the man's rather small mouth. "Winston," he reminded her.

Brianna inclined her head obligingly.

"Winston," she corrected herself. "We definitely have no desire to upset you. At the moment, we'd just like to establish a few basic things."

Winston nodded a number of times as he listened to Brianna. "Yes, of course, I quite understand. What can I do to help?"

Jackson thought back to what he'd heard his temporary partner tell Del Campo. It was a good place to start.

"We need the hotel's guest ledgers going as far back as possible, plus a list of all the hotel's employees," Jackson said.

Winston appeared mystified. "You do understand that the hotel is over half a century old."

"We are aware of that, yes, sir," Brianna answered.

The billionaire's next question was unexpected and threw them. "How old are these bodies you say were uncovered?"

You say.

Brianna replayed the question in her head. She wasn't sure if that was just a slip of the tongue on Aurora's part, or if he was deliberately implying that the whole thing was merely trumped-up charges.

Jackson was obviously rubbing off on her, she thought.

"We won't know that until our ME finishes doing the autopsies," Brianna answered the man.

"If it would help move things along, I know several medical examiners in Sacramento," Winston told them. "I could put in a call for you and get them down here by the end of the week, perhaps even sooner."

"That's very kind of you, sir, but the lab has already put out the word in the department. We have several medical examiners on call already. There's no shortage of willing hands," she assured the billionaire. "But thank you for the offer."

Brianna didn't want to risk offending the man or getting on his bad side. Most of all, she didn't want him to think that they were looking at him as a possible suspect. Right now, that wasn't the case—and it might never be, so they were playing it safe. If it turned out differently down the line, she didn't want to put Winston on alert.

"Win, what on earth is going on here? Why is there a sedan parked in front of the house?"

A statuesque blonde, appearing to be between

her late forties and early fifties, came into the library. Sharp green eyes took immediate measure of the two strangers in the room.

"Who are these people?" she asked, glaring at Jackson and Brianna as if they had just invaded her castle and tracked mud all over the highly polished floors.

"Gloria—" Winston, on his feet, extended his arm out toward his wife, indicating that he wanted her to come stand next to him "—I'd like you to say hello to these two fine young detectives."

"Detectives," Gloria Aurora repeated. "Police or private?" she asked in a tone that had icicles attached to it.

"We're with the city's police department, Mrs. Aurora," Brianna told the woman, doing her best not to react to the judgmental tone.

The woman said nothing to either detective. Instead, she turned toward her husband and demanded, "What are they doing here?" When he didn't answer her as quickly as she wanted, Gloria turned on the two people and questioned them herself. "Why are you here?"

Winston cleared his throat. It was obvious that he didn't want his wife to create a scene, especially not in front of the detectives. He and his brothers had been raised to believe that image was everything.

"There's a problem with the hotel," Winston began to explain.

"The hotel," Gloria repeated, almost with loathing. "Didn't I tell you to get rid of that old relic years ago? Why he hung on to it I'll never know," she said, addressing her words to Jackson. "The man's just too sentimental for his own good. I swear he has a heart like a bowl of mush sometimes. You'd never guess that he's considered to be such a shrewd businessman by his competitors." Mrs. Aurora sighed. "If they'd only seen him the way I have."

"Gloria, these detectives are not here to listen to matters concerning our private lives," he said sternly.

"Neither are you, apparently. Why didn't you sell that hotel before now?" his wife demanded.

Not wanting to get in the middle of a family dispute, Jackson picked up on Mrs. Aurora's question. "Why did you pick now to sell it, sir?"

"Because, Detective," Winston replied, "despite the fact that I did want to hold on to it because it had been my grandfather's pride and joy, I felt that it was time to allow the city to continue growing. Coupled with that," he added, slanting a glance toward his wife, "I received an offer I couldn't refuse."

Chapter 4

"Do you know the name of the person who made this offer?" Jackson asked.

Gloria Aurora scowled. Her frown had the ability to transform an attractive face almost into a mask, one that even her husband had been known to be wary of.

"Winnie, don't you think you should have a lawyer present before you answer any more of these people's questions?" Mrs. Aurora's tone was civil, but it was more of a demand than a question.

It was obvious that the woman was more than a little surprised when her husband held his ground, not against the police detectives, but against her suggestion.

"There's no need for lawyers, Gloria," Winston replied amicably. "There's no wrongdoing here." Chuckling, the family patriarch turned to address the two detectives. "You'll have to forgive my wife. I'm afraid she's not very trusting."

Gloria's eyes were as close to blazing as Brianna had ever seen. "And you're too trusting, Winston," the woman snapped.

Brianna exchanged glances with her partner. Was there just trouble in paradise, or did the man's wife know something? Something she wanted hidden?

"Mr. Aurora," Jackson said a bit more forcefully, "who made you the offer?"

"The city," Winston replied mildly, appearing unfazed by his wife's anger.

This felt as if they were tiptoeing through a minefield, Brianna thought. "Anyone in particular from the city?"

"For the answer to that, I'm afraid that you *will* have to speak to my lawyer," Winston told them.

"Finally!" his wife cried triumphantly with a toss of her ever so carefully coiffed hair.

It was obvious that Winston Aurora was not about to let his wife have the last word. "I hated the idea of selling the property, so I turned everything over to Thomas Cahill, senior lawyer at Cahill, Adams and Sons. Call the firm, tell him I sent you. He can give you all the details behind the sale.

Now," he said in a tone indicating that he assumed the subject was closed, "is there anything else?"

"Not at the moment, sir, but we'll let you know if there is," Brianna told the man pleasantly. Her gaze swept over both parties. "Thank you for your time, Mr. and Mrs. Aurora."

"I hope this is the end of your interrogation." Gloria Aurora's tone was cold enough to freeze large cuts of beef.

"If not," Brianna responded politely, not about to be intimidated, "we'll be in touch."

"With our lawyer!" Gloria called after them as they left the library.

"Well, that proves it," Jackson said as they made their way out of the mansion under the head of security's watchful eye.

"Proves what?" Brianna asked.

They went down the half dozen stairs from the front door to the circular driveway. "That money doesn't buy happiness."

Brianna shrugged. "*He* seemed all right."

Jackson glanced in her direction. "I was referring to *Mrs.* Aurora. Every time that woman opened her mouth to talk, I had the impression that she was sucking on a lemon. A really sour lemon," he underscored. "Almost made me feel sorry for her husband."

"Almost?" Brianna questioned as she got into the car.

Jackson laughed shortly. "Hard to feel sorry for

a man who could buy the whole state before noon if he wanted to."

Jackson sounded as if he was sinking farther into a mood, so she tried to kid him out of it. In her opinion, he was an excellent detective, but he was really difficult to get close to. Even after being partnered with him three times, she was still trying to find the chink in his armor.

"Ah, but as you just pointed out," she told him, "money can't buy happiness."

"Yeah, but it can buy a lot of other things," Jackson replied as he started the car.

Was he going anywhere with this, or just complaining in general, Brianna wondered. "What are you getting at? What other things?"

"Like other people's silence." He began to drive toward the main road. "What do you want to bet that we're not going to get any worthwhile information out of Aurora's lawyer—or anyone else connected with this sale or the demolition, for that matter?"

Jackson sounded as if he believed a major conspiracy was going on. "Hey, the owner of the construction company was the one who called the police," Brianna reminded him.

That didn't change his opinion. "That was a spontaneous reaction," he said. "Besides, some of his crew saw those bodies. And that was *then*. It doesn't take all that long to talk to the involved parties and get them to see things differently, change their stories for a price, that sort of thing."

"Don't you think you're getting a little carried away here?" Brianna asked him. "We're talking about the Aurora family, not a drug cartel or crime syndicate."

Jackson glanced at her, and she couldn't quite read his expression. "We'll see."

"Why do you insist on seeing the dark side of everything?" Brianna asked.

"Why do you always insist on seeing the bright side?" he countered.

She'd expected him to come back with that and was prepared. "Because I like having faith in my fellow human being."

His eyes on the road, Jackson made a disparaging sound. "Fastest way to be disappointed, if you ask me, is to have faith in your fellow human being."

Brianna looked at the man driving beside her for a long moment. She knew very little about Jackson Muldare—other than he was an excellent detective—even though they had worked together before. The little she did know, by way of rumor and innuendo, was rather sad and depressing. She debated saying something to him, trying to make him come around.

But before she could open her mouth, Jackson warned, "Don't analyze me, O'Bannon." He never took his eyes off the winding road.

"I didn't say a word," she said, raising her hands in mock surrender.

"You didn't have to," he told her. "I can *feel* you thinking."

"That's quite a talent you have there," she replied, a touch of mocking in her voice.

"It's my survival instinct," he answered in all seriousness.

While he respected the woman as a detective and, yes, maybe even liked her to some extent, he was aware of the reputation she and the rest of her family had. They never met a person they didn't try to bring into their circle and absorb. Whether or not that person was willing didn't seem to matter. The Cavanaughs were firmly convinced that everyone was better off as part of a group.

Hell, most of the time he didn't even really see himself as part of the police force. He certainly didn't feel the need to buddy up to anyone, no matter what anyone thought to the contrary.

His best bet until this was resolved, Jackson felt, was to keep the woman's mind on the case— and off anything personal that might have to do with him.

Having finally arrived at the main road, he glanced in her direction. "Where do you want to go?"

She thought of what Winston Aurora had said just before they left his mansion. "We might as well get the family lawyer out of the way, see if he can shed some light on the sale of the decade."

Jackson laughed shortly, although there was no smile on his face. "I can just see the posting online— 'For sale, one classic hotel. Comes with built-in tenants, no extra charge.'"

"Why, Muldare, I had no idea that you had a sense of humor."

His expression remained unchanged and almost stoic. "I don't."

"That would explain a lot of things," she responded. It occurred to Brianna that she hadn't given him the address to the law firm. "Oh, Cahill's office is located on—"

"I know where it is," he cut her off. And then, in case she had any doubts about what he'd just said, he told her, "McFadden."

Brianna just shook her head. "Muldare, you are just an endless source of surprises, you know that?"

For the first time since they'd left the hotel, she noticed just the barest hint of a smile on Jackson's ruggedly handsome face. "I like keeping you on your toes," he said.

What Muldare liked, she thought, was keeping her off balance.

She paused for a second, debating her next question. Deciding she had nothing to lose, she forged ahead and asked, "How's everything?"

The simple question made no sense to him. He

never liked things that made no sense. "In reference to what?"

"Your life," she specified. Met with a stony silence, she tried again. "I'm asking you about your life, Muldare."

"You writing a book?" he asked her.

"No," she replied, doing her best not to get exasperated. "I'm trying to make small talk with my partner."

"Your *temporary* partner doesn't like small talk," Jackson told her. "It serves no purpose. Hence the word *small*."

He really was an exasperating man, Brianna thought. But she was far too stubborn to give up.

"Then you're missing the point of small talk," she told him.

"Isn't that the lawyer's building just up ahead to the right?" he asked, knowing full well that it was. He only asked because he wanted to divert her attention.

Aware of what he was trying to do, Brianna suppressed a sigh. *This isn't over, Muldare.*

She turned her attention toward the very modern-looking building Jackson had just pointed out. The edifice was constructed out of what looked to be, at first glance, all reflective glass. At certain times of the day in the spring and fall, the building made driving by it close to impossible because of the glare. But since it was only for a few minutes each time, and the office building housed a number of important companies, no steps were taken to change anything.

"That it is," Brianna said, confirming what she knew that Muldare already knew. "Small talk is tabled for now," she said deliberately—and then put him on notice. "But I intend to get back to it."

"Good luck with that," Jackson murmured under his breath.

But she heard him. And she smiled because at that moment, she'd made herself a vow. She fully intended to peel away Jackson Muldare's protective shield if it was the last thing she ever did. Not to satisfy her own curiosity, which she admittedly had in spades, but because she felt that he needed to expose whatever it was he was guarding so zealously to the light of day. She was convinced that he would remain a tortured soul until such time as he cleared out his demons.

Forewarned, Roman Thomas Cahill was waiting for them when they arrived at the law firm.

Stopping at the reception desk, Brianna and Jackson asked the very efficient-looking young man manning the desk if they could speak with Cahill.

"First door to your right," the receptionist said. "Mr. Cahill is waiting for you."

"One hurdle down, four hundred and ninety-nine to go," Brianna said to her partner.

"Only?" was Jackson's response.

A moment later, they were walking into R. Thomas Cahill's cavernous office.

Leaving the shelter of his desk, Cahill met them halfway. "I was told that you'd be stopping by," he said, shaking both their hands. He gestured toward the two chairs before his desk, his indication clear. "Although I must admit that I'm a little unclear why the Aurora police department would have the slightest interest in the sale of the Old Aurora Hotel." He chuckled. "I realize that the city doesn't have much in the way of crime to keep detectives like yourselves busy, but surely there are more pressing things for you to look into than the sale of that fine old building to the city in order to make way for another wave of development." Finished, he leaned back in his richly padded chair, his hands on either armrest as he waited for the weight of his words to sink in.

"Well, that's quite a mouthful, Mr. Cahill," Jackson commented.

Was he deliberately trying to irritate everyone today, Brianna couldn't help wondering. She instantly went into damage control mode.

"What my partner is trying to say," she told the lawyer, "is that we're wondering if you could clarify why the property was sold at this particular time and who on the city council authorized the sale."

Cahill's expression remained unchanged. "Again,

I have to say that I hardly see why that would concern the police department."

Jackson grew tired of all this beating around the bush. "It does if the building in question has bodies in it."

"Bodies?" Cahill echoed. "What the hell are you talking about?"

"When the construction crew began demolishing the hotel this morning, they found bodies in the debris," Jackson answered.

Cahill didn't look as if the news surprised him. Although there was a flash of color on his florid face, it gave way to a thoughtful expression as he advanced a theory. "That's easy enough to explain. There were undoubtedly homeless people living in the building—they turn up everywhere—and they didn't manage to get out in time."

Brianna could see that Jackson was on the verge of losing his temper. Placing her hand lightly on his wrist to placate him, she took the lead.

"No, these bodies didn't belong to any homeless people looking for shelter. These bodies had been encased in cement," Brianna told the lawyer.

Cahill's complexion turned a serious shade of red as he rose to his feet. "Surely you don't mean to sit here and accuse my client of having anything to do with such a heinous crime. Bear in mind that I can and will sue you and your whole department for defamation of character if either of you even so much as breathe this outside my office."

Not about to be intimidated, Brianna and Jackson were on their feet as well.

"Before we get into all that ugliness, Mr. Cahill," Brianna said in a calm voice that seemed to have the exact opposite effect on the attorney, "why don't you just tell us who approached your client about the sale of the Old Aurora Hotel? You tell us that and we will get out of your hair."

"And you can get back to doing whatever it is that lawyers do," Jackson interjected.

"Don't tempt me to show you," Cahill said as he drew himself up to his full height, which was at least five inches shorter than Jackson. Clearly struggling to keep his temper in check, Cahill turned away from Jackson and said to Brianna, "If you'll wait right here, I'll see about getting you that information."

With that, the attorney stormed out of his office.

"Why do you think he didn't use his computer to get that information?" Jackson asked, looking at the door.

"Probably because he wanted to get some space between himself and you before he did something that isn't smiled upon in law school." She looked at the other detective, more amused than annoyed. "Am I going to have to put a leash on you?"

"You can try," Jackson told her. Then, eyeing her for a moment, he added, "Might even be fun to watch you try."

For just a second, an image that had nothing to

do with the case flashed through her mind. *Not the time*, she silently lectured.

"We're trying to make nice with these people," Brianna reminded him. "Haven't you ever heard that it's easier to catch flies with honey than with vinegar? And if you give in to your urge and use a flyswatter," guessing what was going through Jackson's mind, "then you haven't gotten anything at all for your trouble except for a flyswatter full of smashed flies."

Jackson gave her a look she couldn't read. "Anyone ever tell you you're colorful?"

"Muldare, I'm serious," she stressed. "We need these people to cooperate."

A hint of disbelief entered his eyes. "Are you telling me that you expect these people to just raise their hands and say, 'You got me. I did it'?"

"No, what I'm hoping is that one of these people might say something to help us find out just who decided to use the Old Aurora Hotel to cover up their killing spree." She sighed as other thoughts occurred to her, things that needed to be checked out. "We're going to need to get a task force together to help us tackle this."

"Safety in numbers?" Jackson asked.

"Efficiency in numbers," she countered. "I get the feeling that there are a lot of pieces involved in keeping all this secret, and the more people we have working on this, the better chance we stand of getting some answers before someone in the Aurora family tries to stonewall us."

"Then you *do* think it's someone in the family," Jackson asked. His tone made it clear that he already thought that way.

"Until we get a few more things straightened out, I'm not thinking anything just yet," she answered.

Jackson was about to ask her something else when Cahill walked back into the office.

At the same time, Jackson's phone began to vibrate.

Chapter 5

The R. Thomas Cahill who reentered his office bearing the information that had been requested of him bore little resemblance to the man who had initially greeted the two police detectives. He grudgingly placed the single sheet of paper he'd taken out of the printer on the desk in front of Brianna.

"All right, here's the name of the man who spearheaded the authorization to buy the Old Aurora Hotel." Cahill's beefy lips puckered into a frown. "I hope this concludes our business."

"Our business," Jackson said, sliding the sheet of paper closer to him and picking it up, "will be concluded when we find out who killed those people entombed in the hotel walls."

The lawyer squared his shoulders like a soldier bracing for battle. "And when you find that out, I will expect a full apology for my client from both of you."

Brianna took the sheet of paper from her partner and glanced at the name on it. "Thank you for this," she said politely.

With that, she and Jackson left the man's private office and made their way out to the main lobby and the elevators.

Jackson noticed that she'd folded the paper and put it into her shoulder bag. "The name Harold Harris mean anything to you?" he asked Brianna as they got on the elevator.

"Not yet," Brianna answered.

Jackson reached over and pressed the button for the ground floor. She looked at the way Jackson's breast pocket was vibrating. Again.

"Either you're really excited to be on this elevator with me," she commented, "or someone is trying to call you."

The laugh was dry. "Sorry to disappoint you," Jackson said, "but it's my phone."

The elevator car arrived on the ground floor and opened its door. Jackson was the first one out, a clear sign, as far as Brianna was concerned, that he was attempting to avoid her—or at least her questions.

Fat chance, Brianna thought.

"Don't you want to answer that?" she asked. She

did her best to lengthen her stride in order to catch up to him. Jackson was almost at the car.

"No." The single word, prickly and sharp, hung in the air between them as they reached the car.

"No?" she repeated incredulously. Ringing phones were supposed to be answered. She'd never been able to ignore one herself. "It might be important. You're not even checking to see who's calling."

And then suddenly Brianna said the first thing that occurred to her. "Girlfriend?"

It had to be a girlfriend calling him, otherwise why would Muldare be ducking the call like this? Men could be commitment-shy, and ducking calls was all part of that.

Jackson slanted an impatient look in her direction. "Why don't you put that inquisitive mind of yours to work on solving this case?" Unlocking the door, he got in on the driver's side.

"I can do both," Brianna replied, getting into the passenger side. "On occasion, I've also been known to walk and chew gum at the same time, too."

Jackson shook his head. "Knew there was a reason why they promoted you to detective."

She saw that his breast pocket was vibrating again. It had stopped for a moment when he'd walked out of the elevator. That made three times, by her count.

"She's not giving up," she pointed out, amused.

Starting the vehicle, Jackson pulled out of the

spot and out onto the main thoroughfare. Impatience gave way to mounting annoyance. He shot Brianna a black look.

"It's not a she," he informed her.

"Oh." Even more questions began to fill her head, but she bit them back. Instead, she offered, "Anything I can do to help?"

"You can stop asking questions," he snapped.

The vibrating began again. It was clear that the caller wasn't letting up until Jackson picked up.

"If you want to take that, I can get out of the car while you talk." Muldare just continued driving. "Of course, in order for me to do that, you're going to have to stop the car," Brianna pointed out. "I don't bounce all that well."

Jackson muttered something heated and unintelligible under his breath, then pulled sharply over to the right, temporarily stopping in the bicycle lane.

As he reached inside his pocket for his cell phone, Brianna opened the passenger door, fully intending to get out the way she'd offered. She was surprised when Jackson caught her arm. Turning to look at him, she saw him shake his head at her even as he answered his phone.

"I can't talk now," he said to whoever was on the other line the moment he answered.

Even though she didn't want to eavesdrop, Brianna heard someone pleading, "You've gotta get me out of here, Jack. Please!"

"I'll call you back later," Jackson answered,

measuring out each word as if there was a bitter taste to it.

Whoever was on the other end was saying something in response when Jackson terminated the call. Shoving the cell phone back into his pocket, he started the car and pulled away from the curb.

Brianna gave it a couple of seconds, but he clearly wasn't about to say anything about the call. So she made an offer.

"Look, why don't we go back to the precinct? You drop me off there so I can get my car, or at least another car if Del Campo isn't back, and I'll follow up with Harold Harris while you do what you need to do," she concluded, waving at his phone.

"I *am* doing what I need to do," Jackson informed her tersely. "I'm going with you to talk to this Harold Harris and find out if he knew anything that made him get the city to buy that old hotel."

"I can go there alone," Brianna stressed.

Making a right, Jackson glared at her for one fleeting moment. "The chief of Ds put us together on this for a reason. I've got to believe it's not just so you can nag me."

"I'm not nagging," Brianna cried defensively. "But if you want nagging, Muldare, you ain't seen nothin' yet."

Looking at his profile, she noticed his jaw hardening. He really *did* have chiseled features, she thought—and right now, a heart to match.

"You're not going to ask me who that was?" he asked, referring to his phone call. He was surprised she wasn't grilling him.

Naturally curious, it took everything for her to suppress the urge to ask, but out loud she said, "Only if you want to tell me."

"I don't," he told her flatly.

"Okay then," she replied, trying her best to sound as if she was all right with that arrangement.

Brianna looked out the window, biting her lower lip. Telling herself she was doing the right thing.

She lasted for three and a half blocks.

"All right, damn it, who was that?" she asked.

"What happened to 'only if you want to tell me'?" Jackson asked.

"I lied," she admitted. "I *want* you to tell me. Who *was* that on the phone?"

Jackson sighed, keeping his eyes on the road, not trusting himself to look at her right now. He was an exceptionally private person, and part of him was all set to dig in.

But oddly enough, there was a small part that wanted the release of sharing this burden, even if logically he knew there was nothing she could do or say about it that would help in the slightest.

Maybe he was losing it.

"My brother." The two words came out grudgingly.

Now that Muldare had opened the door, more

questions just came pouring out. "Where is he? Why does he want you to get him out?"

Jackson shook his head. He should have known better than to say anything, he thought. "Damn, I really miss those clamshell phones." If he'd had one of those, chances were good that she wouldn't have been able to overhear Jimmy's pleading.

Brianna shifted in her seat to face him squarely. "Jackson, I'm serious. Drop me off at the station. If you need to go to your brother, do it," she urged.

Damn it, he should have just kept his mouth shut. "You're not going to stop, are you?"

"He's your brother and he obviously needs you," she said. "I'm part of a big family and I know all about being there for a sibling. I've been on both sides of that—needing and being needed."

For a moment he debated telling her that none of this was her business, but he knew O'Bannon was only concerned. It wasn't something he was used to, but apparently it was a big thing in the world she lived in.

For just a split second, he wondered what it must have been like, growing up in her world. A sliver of envy pricked him.

Giving in to the inevitable—and maybe hoping for a little peace—he told her, "My brother's an addict and he's in rehab. He doesn't want to be there, but that's where he's going to stay until he can get through a day without numbing the hell out of his mind with any drug he can get his hands on."

His voice was hard. It came from hardening himself in order not to give in to his brother's begging and pleading. It also came from turning a deaf ear to the scores of promises he'd heard from Jimmy, promises to "do better next time."

"I put him there and he's going to stay there until he's kicked his habit. Any more questions?" he snapped.

"Just one," Brianna answered quietly, holding up an index finger. When he looked at her, she said, "Why the hell have you been carrying this bottled up inside you without telling me?"

He would have glared at her if he didn't have to keep his eyes on the road. "What the hell are you talking about? They just put us together on this case."

That was just an excuse and he knew it, she thought. "But this isn't our first time working together." When he said nothing in response, Brianna tried again, reminding him, "We've gone out for drinks."

"*I* went out for a drink," he corrected. "You just happened to be there." As expected, she'd found a way to strew rose petals all over and cloud the issue, Jackson thought, annoyed with himself for saying anything to her.

Brianna sighed. "You really make it hard to be your friend."

Where the hell had that come from? "I'm not asking you to be my friend," he told her.

"Too bad," she responded with a laugh. "You're stuck with me."

Again, he knew she meant well, but this was a doomed venture on her part. Didn't she understand that? Because he did like her in his own way, he tried to make her understand. "Look, O'Bannon, I'm not a touchy-feely type person—"

Brianna raised her hands as if to underscore her statement. "No touching, no feeling, just talking."

They stopped at a light, and this time he did look at her. The woman was impossible. "Do you know if they have any openings in the K-9 unit?"

He saw her smile spread; somehow it seemed to take over her entire expression, like a morning sunrise.

"Sorry, you're out of luck. No openings. Don't worry," she told him kindly. "You don't have to talk to me right now."

"Thank God."

You are not going to put me off, Jackson Muldare, no matter how hard you try, she silently vowed.

"But I'm here when you need me."

Pressing down on the accelerator, Jackson just barely made it through a yellow light before it turned red. "Does the phrase *when hell freezes over* mean anything to you, O'Bannon?"

"Nope." Brianna suddenly turned in her seat, looking to her right as he drove by the police station. "Hey!" she cried, raising her voice. "You just passed the precinct, Muldare."

"I know," he answered, unfazed. "We're going to city hall."

"But—" Her protest froze and then she sighed, sinking back into her seat. "You know, you're as stubborn as I am."

Although he never liked being compared to anyone or anything, he had to admit this one had some merit. And, oddly enough, it didn't bother him.

"I guess that's what makes this interesting," he responded.

Harold Harris was on the premises and available when Jackson and Brianna asked to speak with him. Moreover, they found that he was more than happy to see them and answer their questions.

According to the councilman, he and some of his fellow council members thought that the Old Aurora Hotel's time had come and gone. Legend had it that the building had been constructed to resemble a sprawling Southern mansion in homage to George Aurora's place of birth, a small town just outside Raleigh, North Carolina. Because it had weathered badly and looked as if it was ready to fall apart, Harris felt that the land it was standing on could be put to far better use.

That was when, he proudly told them, the salesman in him took over.

"Have you seen the view from there?" he asked.

"You *have* to go see it," he urged. "It's absolutely breathtaking. Homes here are selling at a premium right now—faster than you can blink," he stressed. "These proposed homes will be scooped up before the builder even has the land fully graded and mapped out to start work."

"Is that why you urged the council to put a bid on the hotel?" Brianna asked. "Because of the view?"

The man bobbed his head up and down, sun-bleached hair falling into his eyes. "I have an eye for things like that," he told them and then couldn't help confiding, "I really can't wait for the groundbreaking ceremony."

Seeing the man's eagerness, she almost hated bursting his bubble. Unlike Aurora's lawyer, this man actually seemed genuine to her.

"I'm afraid you're going to have to wait a little longer than you've anticipated," Brianna told him.

Confusion entered the man's gray eyes. "I don't understand," Harris said, his wide smile fading a little around the edges. "Why's that? The demolition crew started early this morning."

Brianna was surprised that word about the stoppage hadn't reached the council yet. She was about to tell him when Jackson spared her the ordeal.

"That's just the problem," Jackson told the councilman matter-of-factly. "As soon as the walls started coming down, bodies began falling out." He knew he was stating it rather simplistically, but that was the general gist of it.

Harris stared at him as if the detective had suddenly lapsed into some strange foreign language.

"You're joking," he practically choked out.

"I only wish we were, Mr. Harris," Brianna said, stepping in. "And until the investigation yields some concrete—no pun intended—answers, I'm afraid that all work on the site will have to be on hold."

Harris turned pale. "Is there any way around that?" he asked, distressed.

"Not unless you can tell us who killed these people and how they wound up being part of the architecture," Jackson said.

"I ca-can't," Harris stuttered, his eyes moving like tennis balls from Brianna to Jackson, then back again. "How would I possibly know that?"

"If I could answer that, Mr. Harris, this whole conversation would be moot," Brianna told him kindly.

But rather than go away, Harris's panic only intensified. "You don't understand. I talked the council into this. Every day that the project isn't started, we're hemorrhaging money."

She really did feel sorry for the man. "We're trying to get to the bottom of this as quickly as possible," she assured the councilman, who was now visibly perspiring.

Her assurance didn't help. The man continued looking ghostly white.

"Try harder," he implored. As Brianna and Jackson rose to their feet, Harris said, "You'll keep me posted about this and tell me the minute we can begin work?"

"You'll be our first call," Brianna promised just before they left.

"Why did you lie to him?" Jackson asked, curious. Of the two of them, he would have said that she was the do-gooder while he was the one who didn't give a damn about public relations, and yet she had clearly lied to the councilman. He was definitely *not* going to be the first one they notified, or even the fifth person. There was protocol to follow.

They were outside now, and as Brianna glanced up, she saw clouds gathering.

"Because I hate to see a grown man cry and he was about as close to that as I've seen in a long time," she told Jackson. "Besides, it gives him something to hang on to, and he looked like he really needed that."

Jackson drew his own conclusions from her ostensibly charitable actions. "So you don't think he had anything to do with this creative cemetery?"

"Other than being greedy and somehow making money on the deal, no, I don't think he's mixed up in this—at least for now, anyway," she amended. "I'm willing to be shown the error of my ways if it turns out that I'm wrong," she added. "But for now, I think we need to look elsewhere for our answers—and the killer. Or killers, as the case may be." She looked at Jackson over the roof of his sedan, one hand on the passenger door handle. "This really is a mess, isn't it?"

He laughed shortly. "Yeah. To quote Oliver Hardy talking to Stan Laurel, 'Well, this is another fine mess you've gotten me into.'"

Brianna's eyebrows drew together in a delicately sculpted furrow of confusion. "Who?"

Jackson shook his head. "Never mind." He opened the door on his side. "Just get in the car."

But she remained where she was, trying to get to the bottom of the quotation he'd just carelessly tossed at her. "No, really, am I supposed to know who those people are? Is that a reference to something out of your past?"

He thought back to a childhood with a black-and-white TV set rescued out of a Dumpster and used to entertain his brother to keep Jimmy from crying for the mother who had abandoned them. He and Jimmy had watched classic films on some now-defunct channel. Laurel and Hardy had been prominently featured—but he wasn't about to tell O'Bannon any of that. No telling when she'd bring it up.

"Just get in the car, or run alongside it while I drive. I don't care. Take your pick," he said, getting in behind the steering wheel.

"Getting in," she announced as he turned on the ignition.

"Good choice."

Chapter 6

Walking into the squad room, Brianna saw that her regular partner, Francisco Del Campo, was back at his desk. He appeared to be working on something on his computer.

"Hopefully, that's a good sign," she commented to Jackson.

When he made no response, she glanced over her shoulder and saw that Jackson wasn't listening. Instead, he seemed to be scanning the immediate area as if he was looking for something.

"Can I help you find something?" she asked him.

"Some place to sit might be helpful," he answered, still looking around.

"And I suppose you want a desk to go with that," Brianna quipped.

Jackson stopped scanning the area and instead glanced at her. "I see that you still have that droll sense of humor."

"I've got something better than that. I've got a chair *and* a desk for you. It's right over there." She pointed to it. "Come with me."

He fell into place behind her. "Don't have much choice, do I?"

"Nope." She led Jackson over to a desk a couple of aisles over from her own. Gesturing toward it, she asked, "How's this?"

Jackson surveyed the desk. "Isn't someone sitting there?"

"Yes, you, for the next two weeks," Brianna answered.

He frowned. "How about the person who goes with the papers, the books and those photos over there?" he asked, gesturing toward a couple of framed photographs on the side of the desk.

"That would be Will Jefferies. Right now he's at a seminar, his eyes glazing over, for a week, and then he goes on vacation for another week."

Jackson eyed her skeptically. "So you think we're solving this in two weeks?"

"Hopefully," Brianna responded. "If not, then we'll find another empty desk for you. And we'll keep on finding empty desks until we solve this damn thing." She saw Jackson dubiously eyeing the cluttered desk. "Just put all that either on the floor or in the drawers. He's certainly not going to mind."

"What about his computer?" Jackson pointed out. "Isn't it password protected?"

Brianna pressed her lips together to suppress a laugh. "Jefferies wouldn't know a password if it bit him. That's part of the reason he's away, taking that seminar." That problem solved, she began to turn away. "I'll let you get settled in. I need to talk to Del Campo to find out if he had any luck tracking down the hotel's last guest lists."

"Wait," he called after her. She stopped and half turned, waiting. "Settling in will take me less than five minutes," he said. "What do you want me to do after that?"

A smile slowly spread across her lips. "You could try calling your brother back."

Brianna walked away before he could respond to that. She was fairly sure that he wasn't going to respond happily or politely.

"Any luck, Francisco?" Brianna asked as she approached Del Campo's desk.

The detective swung his chair away from his computer to look at Brianna. The eight-year veteran of the force looked rather pleased with himself.

"Some," he answered. "I tracked down the hotel's last assistant manager. And before you ask, the hotel's last manager died in a car accident a year and a half ago, so he wasn't available for comment."

"Not without a séance," she quipped. "So, what did you get from the assistant manager?"

Del Campo laughed drily. "You mean besides attitude?"

"Why attitude?" she asked, perplexed.

Del Campo handled himself rather well. Unlike some detectives, he knew how to ask questions and get people talking, so the attitude couldn't be in response to questions that Del Campo had asked.

"Suffice to say that Ryan Holt—that's the assistant manager—didn't have any glowing words of praise for the hotel's owners."

"Owners?" Brianna repeated. "Plural? I thought the hotel belonged to Winston Aurora."

"Turns out that it belonged to all three of the Aurora brothers," Del Campo informed her. "And they're not quite as generous to their employees as they would like the world at large to believe.

"Half the time I talked with Holt, he was complaining about how small his salary had been, making the monthly pension he's receiving now pretty paltry. Seems he wasn't too keen about the benefits the Auroras paid their employees, either."

She rested a hip on the corner of his desk, crossing her arms before her as she took the information in. "Do you think he might have been responsible for sealing in those bodies into the hotel walls?" she asked Del Campo. "Wouldn't be the first time a disgruntled employee got back at his bosses by framing them for some kind of a crime."

Francisco shook his head. "Not unless he had someone else doing the heavy work for him. The guy's built like a giant toothpick. He would have had trouble dragging a five-pound bag of potatoes ten feet, much less depositing it behind a wall."

Okay, so they'd struck out there. "Did he offer up *anything* useful?"

"Oh, yeah!" Del Campo answered with enthusiasm. "Seems that the guy hung on to every scrap of paper he put his name to when he worked at the hotel. I've got a ledger with the names of the last five years' worth of guests to stay in it." A wide smile broke out. "Hey, this might interest you," he told her, thumbing through the pages until he found what he was looking for. "Two of the guests in that ledger were permanent."

She wasn't sure what he meant by that. "You mean that they had rooms reserved for them year-round?"

"No, they were *in* hotel rooms year-round," Del Campo told her. Then he explained, "They lived in the hotel instead of in an apartment or house."

"That's kind of expensive," she commented. "Not to mention kind of transient."

"Well, it's definitely too rich for me, but not for people who have money and enjoy being pampered and fussed over. Think about it. Someone makes your bed for you every day and cleans your suite the second you go out. You get room service if you don't feel like eating in the hotel dining room. You don't have to cook ever again. Hell, there are people who live on cruise ships all year round. Here at least you don't risk getting seasick—or, more important, sinking," he emphasized.

Brianna laughed as she shook her head. That way of life definitely did *not* appeal to her. Living in a hotel room or on a cruise ship would make her feel completely rootless.

"Different strokes for different folks, I guess." Getting off the desk, she picked up the list Del Campo had written up for her. She briefly looked over the names. "Good work, Francisco."

"Speaking of work, how's it going with Major Crimes over there?" Del Campo nodded his head in Jackson's general direction.

She looked over toward Jackson, although she really didn't need to. "I've worked with him before."

"You're not answering my question," Del Campo pointed out.

She supposed she wasn't, but she wasn't about to say anything critical about Muldare. That would throw a wrench into the works.

"He's different," Brianna allowed. "Listen, Francisco, can you find something out about Muldare's background for me?"

His curiosity piqued, Del Campo moved closer toward her. "What do you want to know?"

"Anything," she emphasized. "Family background, just things like that," she answered, deliberately keeping her request vague. This business with his brother had made her curious.

Del Campo looked at her, puzzled. "What does this have to do with the case?"

"Nothing," Brianna admitted. It had absolutely nothing to do with the case they were investigating, just the man she was investigating it with. "Just my curiosity kicking in."

Del Campo laughed at her answer. "You mean just your Cavanaugh kicking in." When he saw a trace of annoyance crease her brow, he said, "I know all about your family, Bri. You all have this idealistic notion that everybody's supposed to be happy and connecting with everybody else. You know, it doesn't always work that way, partner."

She didn't care for being analyzed, even by someone she liked. "Just get me the information whenever you can—in your spare time," Brianna threw in to make it sound casual.

Del Campo almost laughed in her face. "Yeah, like I know what *that* is," he said as Brianna walked away.

"Whenever," she tossed over her shoulder.

When Brianna returned to her desk, Jackson was already there, waiting for her.

"Did you get a list of former hotel guests from Del Campo?"

She placed the list Del Campo had typed up for her on her desk so that Jackson could look at it.

"Right here," she answered, pushing it closer to him. "Did you call your brother?"

Jackson never looked up. "He wasn't a guest at the hotel."

She blew out a breath. Why did everything always have to be so difficult with him? But then, she reminded herself, she'd been raised on difficult. She had three older brothers. "You know what I mean, Muldare."

He murmured something under his breath, then said, "Unfortunately, yes, I do. But that's a private matter and we're here during business hours," he reminded her. "Which means we need to be taking care of business. And I've got a feeling that everyone wants to see this case resolved and placed in a nice little box with a tight lid on it. The sooner, the better," Jackson emphasized.

The problem was, Jackson wasn't wrong, Brianna thought. It took very little imagination for her to envision the mayor getting involved in this. The Auroras were essentially the city's founding fathers, and as such, the family was a very big deal in the *city* of Aurora.

They contributed to all the local charities as well as to the police and fire departments. Whatever needed doing, if there weren't sufficient funds in the city's coffers to get it done, the Aurora family could always be counted on to open their wallets in order to cover the expenses. No one wanted to offend them.

But what about the people who weren't able to speak for themselves? What about the people whose bodies had been uncovered in the rubble that the wrecking ball had brought down? Granted, they—or what was left of them—were past being offended. But not past being avenged.

Brianna took a deep breath, struggling not to work herself up.

She didn't realize that Jackson had been talking to her until she felt his hand on her shoulder. Coming around, she almost jumped as she turned to look at him.

"Earth to O'Bannon." The way Jackson said the phrase to her, Brianna knew it wasn't the first time he had tried to get her attention.

"What?" she asked, trying to appear in the moment—as if she hadn't somehow misplaced the last couple of minutes while she'd been lost in thought.

"Are you back now?" he asked, something akin to amusement on his face.

"Sorry. Just tell me what you were saying," she retorted shortly.

He inclined his head obligingly. "I said, do you want to start looking for the people on that list so we can question them, or do you want to go to the morgue to see if the ME has anything useful to tell us yet?"

The man definitely did not have a gift for words, she thought.

"We can swing by the morgue first," she told Jackson. "But when we talk to the ME, do yourself a favor and leave out the word *useful*, okay?"

He wasn't following her, something, he was beginning to recall, that happened on a fairly regular basis. The woman had a way of messing with his mind and distracting him, not just because of what she said, but the way she looked when she said it. He had to force himself to focus on the words and not the woman saying them. "What?"

"You make it sound as if you're talking down to a person when you phrase it like that."

"I have no idea what you're talking about," Jackson said, exasperated.

"All right," she said, finding it difficult to remain delicate. "I'll put it another way. You need people lessons, Muldare."

"I know how to do my job," Jackson retorted, ticked off by her criticism.

"I didn't say you didn't know how to do your job," she protested. "As a matter of fact, Muldare, you're a great cop. But you have a knack for rubbing people the wrong way."

This was getting to be tiresome, and he made no effort to hide his feelings from her.

"I'm not in it to rub people the right way," he informed her. "I'm in it to keep people from getting killed by the bad guys—and to find out who did it if they are."

"You'll be able to do your job a lot quicker and

get a lot more cooperation from people if you don't make those people have to fight the urge to go after you with pitchforks and torches."

"So you say," he replied wearily, just wanting to put an end to this annoying discussion she seemed to feel duty bound to have with him. "You want me to drive to the morgue?" he asked Brianna.

He was missing her point about being nice to other people, but he was being polite to her—in a fashion. She took what she could get and hoped that would open the door to more.

"See, that wasn't so hard now, was it, Muldare?" she asked.

Jackson shook his head, doing his best to hang on to the frayed ends of his temper. She had the ability to get under his skin and get him to lose his temper faster than anyone else he'd ever dealt with.

"You know, half the time I don't know what you're talking about, O'Bannon. The other half of the time, I *wish* I didn't," he told her wearily.

"And it only gets better with time, trust me," a tall, dark-haired detective said to Jackson as he passed them.

Jackson turned to look at the detective quizzically. "Do I know you?" But the man just continued walking to the other side of the squad room.

"Nobody asked for your input, Ronan," Brianna called out. "I don't need you spooking my partner."

"I take it that *you* know him," Jackson assumed as they walked out of the squad room.

"Only vaguely," Brianna answered, then after a beat, added, "He's my oldest brother."

"So why aren't you working this case with him?" Jackson asked. It didn't make sense to have him brought in from another department.

"I just told you why. Because he's my oldest brother." She flashed Jackson a smile. "The trouble with older brothers is that they still see you as being five years old—even if you're a homicide detective with an excellent track record," she added before Jackson could say anything further.

"You have another brother here, too, don't you?" he asked.

"Two more, actually," she answered. "And a sister. And before you ask, I have about a thousand cousins in the police department, too," she told him as she got on the elevator.

"Damn, this really is a family business, isn't it?" Jackson commented, less than comfortable with what that suggested.

The magnitude of what he had just said hadn't fully hit him until just now. Jackson had always been vaguely aware, ever since he had transferred from Oakland and joined the Aurora police force, that there were Cavanaughs in practically every department. However, just how many Cavanaughs there were had never really sunk in before.

"Just keeping the city we love safe," Brianna told him.

Jackson surprised her by asking her a question

that no one else had ever raised. "Having all those relatives around, watching you, doesn't that make you afraid of messing up?"

"You mean because I'm a Cavanaugh?" she questioned. "No. But because I'm a cop, yes," she said. When he looked puzzled, she explained, "It doesn't matter that I'm related to them. What matters is that cops aren't supposed to mess up. We're supposed to make things right."

Unbelievable, Jackson thought, shaking his head as they went outside. "Damn, I didn't know that I was working with Dudley Do-Right."

Unlike his last out-of-the-blue comment about Hardy and Laurel or whoever, this was a reference she was familiar with.

"Dudley didn't have curves," she countered, recalling watching the less-than-stellar antics of the cartoon Mountie.

"I never watched the cartoon that closely," Jackson replied drily.

"Obviously. By the way," she said as they approached the rear parking lot, "you can drive us to the morgue—unless you'd rather I did," she told him.

She was kidding, right? Given a choice, he would always opt to be behind the wheel. The truth was, he didn't trust anyone else's driving but his own. "I'll drive."

"Thought you might say that," Brianna commented with a smile.

Chapter 7

Brianna felt almost overwhelmed the moment she and Jackson stepped into the city's morgue.

Admittedly, Brianna didn't come here very often. And when she did, it was usually when Kristin was on duty. Her main reason for dropping by then was to see if her cousin's wife wanted to grab some lunch.

But she could not recall a single instance when the morgue had *ever* looked even half this busy.

Ordinarily there was only one medical examiner on duty. On occasion, there might be an aide on the premises to help assist the ME. This time, however, there were three medical examiners, counting Kristin, all carefully working over bits and pieces of remains that bore more resemblance to scattered chicken bones than to actual human bodies.

Brianna looked more closely. Not only were the medical examiners working to reconstruct badly decomposed remains, but there seemed to be more than the usual number of gurneys spread all throughout the morgue. Ten in all. And all the gurneys had greater or lesser piles of bones spread out on them waiting to be put together like macabre jigsaw puzzles.

She and Jackson had already walked across the large, temperature-controlled room and were almost at her elbow when Dr. Kristin Alberghetti-Cavanaugh, dressed in scrubs like the rest of her team, sensed their presence and looked up.

"Hi. Pull up a gurney and try your luck," Kristin invited, referring to matching up the body pieces. She was only half kidding.

"Speaking of luck," Brianna said, "have you or anyone on your team had any figuring out approximately when these victims were killed?" She assumed that they had to have met with some sort of foul play—there were just too many bodies for this to be anything else.

"Funny you should ask," Kristin responded. Pausing for a second, she looked closer at the man who had come in with Brianna. "New partner?" she asked Brianna.

"Just temporary," Jackson responded.

"Well, Just Temporary," Kristin said, a smile

curving her mouth, "welcome to the morgue. It's not usually this crowded *or* this challenging here," the chief medical examiner told him.

Brianna decided to get the introductions out of the way so they could get back to the real reason they were here. She gestured toward Kristin first. "Dr. Kristin Alberghetti-Cavanaugh, meet Detective Jackson Muldare. He's on loan from major crimes." Kristin smiled a greeting and Jackson nodded in return. "Okay, back to what you started to say," Brianna finished.

For a second, between the piecemeal bodies and the new detective in her morgue, Kristin momentarily lost the thread of her previous thought. "Which was?"

"When I asked if you'd had any luck with these bodies, you said, and I quote, 'Funny you should ask.' What did you mean by that?"

Kristin remembered now. "All right, now bear in mind that this is all just preliminary and other factors might have to be taken into account down the line that could change the results—"

"Spit it out already, Kris," Brianna interrupted.

"Classy," Jackson commented under his breath.

Brianna shot the other detective a disapproving look even as she ignored the sarcasm—or attempted to. "The preliminary findings?" she asked impatiently.

"*Very* preliminary," Kristin emphasized. "So

far, it looks as if we might have bodies from two different eras."

"Two different eras?" Jackson questioned, a look of confusion furrowing his brow.

Kristin stopped to remove her mask so that they could hear her better. Drawing them over to a gurney parked to the far right, she told the two detectives, "For instance, the body on this gurney—or as much of the body as we could put together so far," she qualified, because it clearly was not an entire cadaver, "has been dead for about forty years, give or take a couple of years. As has that one—" she pointed to another gurney that contained three-quarters of a skeleton "—and that one." Kristin gestured toward a gurney holding only enough parts to re-create half a body.

Brianna tried to piece together what the other woman was telling them. "So what you're saying is that we're looking for a killer who isn't killing people anymore."

But Kristin shook her head. "No. Unfortunately, I'm not saying that."

Jackson held up his hand, symbolically calling for a time-out. "But you just said that the bodies have been dead for about forty years or so."

"Those have," Kristin agreed, then crossed over to a gurney she had just moved aside. "But she hasn't."

Now that they looked more closely, it was obvious that the body on this gurney was far less decomposed than the others Kristin had just pointed out to them.

"Is it possible that this one doesn't belong with the others?" Jackson asked. "You know, someone killed her and just needed a convenient, out-of-the-way place to leave the body, so they dumped her in the abandoned hotel, thinking no one would be the wiser?"

"It's possible," Kristin said. "But then how do you explain that one? And that one?" Each time she asked, the medical examiner pointed to another body on a different gurney. "They've all been killed in the last year or so."

This was getting complicated, Brianna thought, frustrated. "Are we talking about a killer who stopped killing, then decided to get back in the game a full generation later?" she asked Kristin.

Kristin sighed. "Frankly, I don't know what we're talking about," she admitted.

Jackson surveyed the ten gurneys. "Is this all of them?" he asked.

"You'd think so, wouldn't you?" Jim Henderson, another one of the MEs, responded.

Jackson and Brianna turned to look at Kristin.

"There's more?" Jackson asked.

"There's more," Kristin answered wearily. "We've got them laid out on gurneys in the next room."

Jackson was almost afraid to ask the medical examiner. "How many?"

"Hard to say," Kristin answered. "We've got a

lot of mismatched pieces on the gurneys, but it looks like there're three to five more bodies. Plus the CSI team still hasn't finished sifting through all the rubble," she informed them. "There were bodies hidden in a number of what looked to be the foundation walls."

The chief medical examiner's eyes swept over the gurneys that were in the main room with them and she sighed wearily.

"I am going to need a very long shower after this is over. I might even start a brand-new water shortage," she speculated.

"No one could blame you," Brianna told her with conviction. She shook her head as she looked at the gurneys. What kind of a loathsome monster did this kind of thing and went on breathing? "Well, keep us posted," she told Kristin.

"Don't worry, I will," Kristin promised. And then, before she got back to work, she added, "You and everybody else who keeps checking up on our progress." She moved in a little closer to the detectives, lowering her voice. "Between you and me, I've never had so many people breathing down my neck in such a short amount of time."

Brianna smiled sympathetically at her cousin's wife. "I'd offer to help," she said, looking around at the various gurneys again, "but I was never any good at jigsaw puzzles."

Kristin laughed shortly. "Neither was I until I

came here. It's amazing what you find you can do when you have to."

"What's your ratio?" Jackson asked. When both the ME and Brianna looked at him with confusion, he explained, "Old bodies to new. How many are there?"

"So far, three new, seven old. But like I said, there are more bodies in the next room. And most likely there are even more on the way," Kristin added with a grim expression.

"Something to live for," Jackson murmured cryptically.

As he said that, his cell phone began to vibrate again. He was sorely tempted to shut off his phone, but he knew that he couldn't do that. Not because he was on the job. He was certain if his superiors wanted to reach him and couldn't, they'd simply call O'Bannon.

The reason he couldn't shut off his phone was the off chance that his father or someone at Happy Pines might be trying to get in touch with him. His father had already had one stroke fairly recently. He'd recovered from it and was still fully functional as far as mobility went. But the next time around, Ethan might not be that lucky.

However, one glance at his phone's screen told Jackson that the persistent caller had nothing to do with his father's health.

He ignored the vibrating phone and looked at Brianna. "We done here for now?"

Rather than answer him, Brianna turned toward Kristin. "You should have seen what he was like *before* I sent him to charm school. Yes," she said, turning back to Jackson, "we're done here. Call me if you have *anything* new to add," she stressed again, glancing at Kristin. "Night or day, doesn't matter when. Call me."

"You got it," Kristin answered. "Nice meeting you, Jackson," she called after the departing detective, raising her voice.

Jackson paused before the morgue's threshold for a second. "Yeah, you too," he replied in a surprisingly sociable tone.

"Nice effort," Brianna commented quietly just after they left the morgue.

"If I were in her place," Jackson responded as they made their way to the elevator, "knee-deep in decomposing body parts, I would have been snapping everybody's head off who came within ten feet of me. She was being nice. Least I could do was be civil. After all," he said, getting into the elevator and pressing the button for the first floor, "I can't let those charm-school lessons go to waste."

It was hard to miss the sarcasm. "You think I went too far," Brianna guessed.

"You?" The elevator door opened and Jackson held it in place as she exited first. He followed her. "Never."

Brianna nodded. "Point taken." Leaving the

square building, they returned to the parking lot. "If I hurt your feelings, I'm sorry."

He didn't bother to look at her. "I have no feelings," Jackson informed her with a dismissive shrug of his shoulders.

They'd parked his vehicle close to the building's entrance and crossed the lot to it now.

"There was a time I would have agreed with you, but I'm not totally sure about that anymore," Brianna admitted.

Getting into his vehicle, she buckled up, then looked at her watch as Jackson started the car. "It's getting kind of late, and I don't know about you, but I'm getting really hungry. We haven't stopped to eat all day. What do you say we grab something at Malone's and call it a day? A few more hours isn't going to make a difference. We can get a fresh start tomorrow, tracking down those old hotel guests to see if any of them can shed some light on what was going on in that hotel all those years."

They were on the main thoroughfare now. "Are you asking me or telling me?"

"Take your pick. Whatever'll get us to Malone's faster has my vote. And if it helps to clear things up for you," she added, "I am lead on this, but we are partners and I've never been the type who throws her weight around."

"So you wouldn't mind if I said no?" Jackson asked, his expression totally unreadable.

Brianna smiled. "I didn't say that."

He nodded. That was what he thought. "Then I guess I'd better not say no."

Her smile widened. "Good choice, Muldare. Drop me off at the precinct. I need to stop off in the squad room and check with Del Campo to see if there's anything new and pressing that came up. If we're in the clear for the night, I'll meet you at Malone's."

"About that," he said, his voice trailing off as he took a right turn toward the police station.

She knew what he was going to say. "You don't want to go to Malone's. Okay, I'm not unreasonable. I'm open for someplace else."

"That's not the point," Jackson told her. Obviously, he didn't want to go anywhere for drinks or for food. He just wanted to be left alone.

But Brianna had no intentions of letting her temporary partner wiggle out of at least having drinks with her. She had already made up her mind that the man needed socializing, and Malone's was the place where police officers and detectives alike threw back a drink and threw off the heavy shackles of depression that the job sometimes snapped on them.

"Look, Muldare, I know for a fact that you do eat on occasion and I'm fairly sure that your cupboard probably rivals Old Mother Hubbard's—" Brianna began, about to launch into what she hoped was a persuasive argument.

Jackson pulled his vehicle into the rear parking lot, coming to a stop near her car. He glared at her, confused. "Who?"

"It's a nursery rhyme," she prompted. "You know, 'Old Mother Hubbard went to the cupboard to get her poor dog a bone—'" She stopped when she saw that her reference and the recitation was going right over his head. "Guess you're not the only one who can come up with obscure references. My point was that you probably don't have anything edible in your refrigerator or pantry, which is why I'm saying we should grab something to eat once we leave here."

"Have you always had this smothering-mothering attitude, or is that something I just seem to bring out in you?" he asked, doing his best not to tell her what she could do with those mothering instincts surfacing.

"Let me put it to you this way," she told him patiently. "Right now you're my partner, which means you're supposed to have my six. You can't do that if you wind up passing out from malnutrition."

Jackson sighed as he waited for the bossiest woman he knew to get out of his car. "I guess you'll meet me at Malone's, then," he said.

Brianna slid out, then paused for a second to look into the car. She smiled at Jackson. "See how easy that was?"

"Not hardly" was his response. The moment she closed the door, Jackson took off.

She stood for a moment, watching as Jackson retraced his path. He drove out of the parking lot and then onto the street that went parallel to the police station. Within a minute, she had lost track of him.

The odds were fifty-fifty that he wouldn't be at Malone's when she got there.

Brianna went up the back stairs to the station's rear entrance. The line about leading a horse to water but not being able to make him drink ran through her mind. It seemed oddly appropriate in this case.

Well, Muldare might not show up tonight. But that didn't mean she would give up. Her mother had taught her a long time ago, by word and example, that nothing was impossible as long as you didn't give up.

And she wasn't about to.

Chapter 8

Brianna spent less than ten minutes in the squad room. She checked in with Del Campo for any updates regarding the hotel's previous guests. At this time, there weren't any. The squad room was almost empty, and her regular partner was just on his way out as well.

"Feel like swinging by Malone's for a beer?" she asked as she sent a copy of the hotel's guest list to her home computer. She wanted to get a head start on locating these people once she got home. There was a sense of urgency humming through her that she just couldn't seem to shake. But she also needed a little downtime as well, which was why she was going to Malone's.

"Do I feel like it?" Del Campo echoed. "Hell yes," the detective said with the enthusiasm of a man who had been envisioning a tall mug of beer shimmering before him all day.

"Okay." Finished, Brianna shut down her machine. "I'm heading there myself and—"

"But I can't," Del Campo injected in a forlorn voice. He trudged to the squad room's threshold like a man who had been drained of all hope. "If I don't get home at a decent hour, Louisa is going to make me sleep in the tub—with the water still in it."

Brianna pressed her lips together, trying not to laugh at the image that created in her mind.

"Sounds pretty soggy. What did you do to get her so angry at you?" She'd met Del Campo's wife on several occasions, and the woman was nothing if not easygoing and sweet.

"Two weeks of coming home late," Del Campo confessed as he reached the hallway.

"You've been doing overtime?" Brianna asked. Did their lieutenant have Del Campo working on another case in his spare time?

"Maybe," Del Campo said vaguely. And then he added, "At Malone's."

Brianna grinned as she joined him at the elevator. "It's starting to all make sense to me."

The elevator door opened, and they both got on. "Louisa wants me to put in some equal time parenting Joey."

"She has a very valid point," Brianna told him. "Go home to your family while you still have one, Francisco." They reached the ground floor and got out. "I'll see you in the morning."

"Sure," he answered sadly. "Have a drink for me—make it a double."

"Beers don't have doubles," Brianna reminded the detective.

"Then make it a *really* tall glass."

It'll probably be a short, quick one, she answered silently as she and Del Campo parted company. Francisco tended to park in the building's front lot while she usually parked in the rear.

Brianna walked back to her car quickly, even though she told herself that there was no real hurry. She doubted that her temporary partner had gone on to Malone's the way she'd suggested. However, she was still going to go there herself. Not for the beer. As far as she was concerned, beer, a necessary evil, was the price she paid for the camaraderie of her fellow police officers.

Her siblings and cousins had a tendency to turn up at Malone's as well. She never knew who would turn up at the bar at any given time, but it was a sure bet that she'd see someone she knew. Kicking back at Malone's was a good way to unwind around people who understood exactly what she was going through.

In the job, there was a certain formality that had to be adhered to, and while she could kid around

with her family members and other police person-
nel she knew, there were still lines that couldn't
be crossed. But at Malone's, there were no lines.
There were only men and women who wore the blue
proudly and who bled the same color as she did.

There was a certain comfort in being around
people like that.

The drive from the precinct to Malone's was
only a couple of blocks. As she approached, she
saw that the bar's parking lot was overflowing, as
was the parking lot of the dry-cleaning business
next door, even though the dry cleaner was closed
for the night.

Driving around, Brianna managed to find what
appeared to be the last available spot in the area.

Malone's was doing very good business tonight.
The establishment was never empty during business hours, but it was usually only teeming like
this on a Friday or Saturday night.

Brianna wondered if her new case had anything to do with the increase of traffic at Malone's.
Maybe finding bodies in the walls and speculating how they got there was, in an eerie way, good
for business.

That was cynical, she silently chided. Maybe Muldare really was rubbing off on her. That couldn't be
good. If anything, she was supposed to be rubbing
off on him, not the other way around.

The wall of noise hit her the second she opened
the door. Brianna paused, catching her breath. It

took her a minute to acclimate to the cacophony of dozens of raised voices, all vying to be heard over one another.

Glancing toward the front of the establishment, she saw one of Malone's newest owners, Dan Reynolds, his face slightly flushed, looking exceedingly happy. Dan was moving rather quickly for a man of his girth. A former police officer, he had a steely look about him despite his smile. It was a look that never really left an officer, even after retirement.

She scanned the immediate area. She knew a lot of the people here tonight, but apparently Muldare was not among them.

She might have known. Next time, she silently promised, she was going to handcuff him and drag him here herself.

A movement behind the bar caught Brianna's eye. When she looked in that direction, she realized that Dan was trying to catch her attention. Once he did, he pointed toward the very back of the establishment. Curious, she turned and glanced in that general direction.

At first, she didn't know what Dan was trying to direct her attention to. Nothing seemed to be out of the ordinary.

And then she saw what Dan was pointing to.

Or rather, whom.

Son of a gun, Brianna thought. *Maybe miracles do happen.*

When she finally reached the small table for two

where Jackson Muldare was sitting, he greeted her with, "I was just about to give up on you. I figured I'd drink your beer, too, and then call it a night."

Brianna looked at her watch as she took the seat opposite him. Talk about being impatient. Not much time had gone by since he'd left the precinct.

"How fast did you think I'd get here?" she asked Jackson.

"Faster than this." He gestured toward the only beer mug that had any brew in it. "I told Dan it was for you, so if it's the wrong brand, blame him."

"I'm not a connoisseur," she assured him. "As long as it's not dark ale, I'm fine with it." Taking a quick sip, she set the mug down again and looked at the table. There was nothing else on it except for his empty beer mug and hers. "You didn't get anything to eat?"

"Anyone ever tell you that you can be pretty demanding?" he asked her.

He was doing it again, trying to distract her from getting an answer to the question she'd asked. "I'm not trying to be demanding—"

"You could have fooled me," Jackson responded philosophically.

Refusing to let him distract her, or worse, to allow thoughts of him to dwell on her mind, Brianna pushed on. "But the whole point of getting you to stop here was so you—we," she corrected before he could make another reference to her acting like a

mother hen, "could get something to eat. Stay here—
I'll go order a couple of hamburgers."

As she pushed back her chair to get up, she all
but bumped into Dan, who was right behind her,
carrying a tray with two hamburgers on it as well
as a basket of fries.

There was amusement on Jackson's face. "You
were saying?"

"That you are a source of constant surprise," she
told him evenly, even though several other descrip-
tive words rose in her mind as well.

"Your friend here said to hold off making the
food until you got here." Dan placed a hamburger
in front of each of them, then put the basket of fries
on the side. "Good thing I'm fast," Dan told Brianna with a touch of pride.

"Good thing," Brianna agreed, flashing a smile
at the retired patrolman.

"Okay, I gotta get back," Dan told them, tucking
the tray under his arm. He looked back toward the
bar and shook his head. "That new bartender my
partner hired looks like he's having trouble keeping up," he said just before he hurried back to the
front of the room.

Brianna turned back toward Jackson. "You
could have told me that you'd ordered the food instead of letting me go on like that."

"And miss seeing your eyes flash like lightning during a summer storm when you really get
going?" Jackson questioned. "Not a chance."

Brianna shook her head as she took her first bite of hamburger. She allowed herself a second to savor the taste before she told Jackson, "You know, I just don't understand you."

He wished she'd stop making everything personal. He didn't want her getting personal. It made maintaining distance between them difficult, and he needed distance in order to function.

"You're not supposed to understand me," he told her. "You're supposed to be trying to understand what would make someone go on a killing spree and then stick all those bodies into the walls. And then, when you've figured that out, figure out *how* he got those bodies in the walls without anyone noticing."

Why was he so afraid of anyone getting close to him? "I can do both," she told him. When Jackson raised one eyebrow in a silent question, she elaborated, "I can try to understand you and figure out why the killer put the bodies there instead of just getting rid of them in some field or ditch."

"Even if you can do both," he told her, "I suggest that you do the latter first. You might have more luck with that, and in any case, that's the important puzzle here, not me."

Her smile was enigmatic, he thought. And maybe just a little bit sexy.

"That's a matter of opinion," she told him.

Well, being subtle wasn't working, he thought.

Maybe he just needed to be blunt. That usually worked better for him, anyway.

"Look, O'Bannon," he said sharply, "I don't want you rooting around in my head, and I don't want you analyzing me. Understood?"

"Understood," she echoed in a dutiful voice.

Jackson frowned at her. She wasn't fooling him for a second. She was just humoring him.

"But you're not going to listen, are you?" he challenged. It was a rhetorical question. He already knew the answer to the question.

Brianna smiled at him. "One right answer out of two isn't bad."

The expression on Jackson's face was dark. He pushed the basket of French fries toward her and retorted, "Eat your fries."

"Only if you do," Brianna countered.

Jackson blew out a long breath, frustrated. He was usually indifferent to the people he worked with. She made him want to strangle her. "Why do you always have to set conditions on everything?"

"I don't," she protested with enough feeling to make him believe that she actually thought she was serious.

Which, upon reflection, made him laugh. "Right," Jackson mocked. "I'm a grown man, O'Bannon. I don't have to be told when to eat or even *if* I should eat."

Since he was missing the point, she explained

it to him. "It's called caring about someone, Muldare."

Caught off guard, Jackson looked at her as if she was crazy. "And why would you *care* about me?" he demanded. "We're strangers."

"We're *not* strangers," she insisted. "We've worked together before."

"Yeah, we've *worked* together," he repeated, emphasizing the word although he could see that she wasn't getting the message. "But that doesn't make us friends."

What he was saying only made her more convinced that she needed to get through to him. "You and I have a different perspective on that," she told him mildly. "Relax, Jackson. What are you afraid of?"

"Strangling a temporary partner," Jackson answered between gritted teeth as he struggled to keep his temper from exploding.

"I'm serious, Muldare," she insisted.

His eyes met hers. "So am I."

Feeling that he was really going to lose his temper at any moment and fairly certain that an entire room full of cops would jump on him for that, he decided to take the safe way out.

Wiping his lips, Jackson dropped his napkin on his plate and rose to his feet. "I'll see you tomorrow, O'Bannon."

She knew what he was doing. He was avoiding a serious conversation with her. But she let it slide. Anything else might result in a scene, which wouldn't benefit either one of them, least of all him.

Brianna nodded. "Okay." And then, as he started to walk toward the front door, she called out, "Don't forget to call your brother."

He didn't turn around and he never lost a step. But he did allow a strange guttural noise that sounded like a cross between an angry bear growling and a coyote howling at the moon to escape his lips.

"Hey, I know that sound," Christian O'Bannon said, sitting down in the seat Jackson had just vacated. The tall, dark-haired detective with liquid green eyes grinned at his younger sister. "That's the sound of someone you've just driven absolutely crazy."

"Nice to see you, too, Chris," Brianna commented. She didn't want to talk about Muldare, even though she could see that her brother did. Pushing the fries toward her brother, Brianna said, "Have a fry."

Christian eyed the half-empty basket. "Is that what he just had?"

"Very funny. If you don't want them, don't have any. More for me," she said, picking up a rather long French fry and popping it into her mouth.

"Heard about the case you just caught," Christian said, taking a fry himself.

"Not exactly breaking news. Apparently everybody in the precinct's heard," she told him.

"Sounds like a real puzzle. If you want any help," Christian went on, specifying, "unofficially, just let me know."

Softening, she smiled. "Thanks. Right now, we don't even know what we don't know," she told him, giving voice to her frustration.

Christian rose, taking a small handful of fries with him. "Then you can only go up from there," he told her with a confident smile.

"If you say so," she sighed.

"I'm serious. If you need any help, just yell." Looking over his shoulder, Christian grinned at her. "As I recall, you were always good at yelling."

"Go," she told him, waving him off. "You're ruining the moment."

"I was never here," he replied just before he made that claim a reality.

Chapter 9

"Well, don't you look bright-eyed and chipper," Francisco Del Campo commented with a knowing grin as he walked into the squad room the following morning and passed Brianna at her desk. He paused to look at her more closely. "I take it last night went well?"

"Last night went exactly the way it should have," she informed him icily. "One beer, one burger, a few fries and then home."

Del Campo was obviously waiting for more. "And then?"

"And then I got to work," she told him. She thought back to the three hours she'd put in, searching for the current locations of the people who were listed as the guests of the Old Aurora Hotel during its last year of business.

"On…?" Del Campo asked, appearing far more interested than she thought he would. She'd had no serious relationship ever since he'd come to work for homicide, and she guessed that he thought she was way overdue. Sitting on the edge of her desk, Francisco leaned forward, determined not to lose a single word.

"The list of hotel guests that you unearthed for me." She sighed, shaking her head as she scrolled down to the next page. "You know, for a guy, you really seem to thrive on gossip."

Del Campo spread his hands and shrugged. "I can't help it. Something's got to add color to my dull life," he said, deliberately sounding mournful. "I'm living vicariously through you and all the other single detectives here."

Brianna laughed drily. "Well, if you're living vicariously through me, you'd better find a way to stay awake through the daytime." She deftly switched topics, getting on more stable ground. "Between last night and this morning, I've managed to track down almost half of these people." She tapped the sheet. "A number of them have either moved out of the county—or, in some cases, they're dead."

"I'll interview the last group," Del Campo volunteered, keeping a straight face.

"Very funny. Speaking of interviews and doing

a little digging…" Brianna said, letting her voice trail off as she looked expectantly at the detective.

"I haven't had a chance to look into that little matter for you," he answered. "Why don't you ask Valri in the computer lab to do it? Legend has it that she can ferret anything out—and isn't she a cousin of yours?"

There were days when she felt as if she was related to the entire police department. Most days that was handy. Some days, it wasn't.

"Yes, but not a close one, and I'd rather not start asking for favors in an official capacity from someone I really don't know all that well." Not unless there was no other way around it.

"Oh, but it's okay to ask me?" Francisco asked, pretending to take offense.

"Sure," Brianna answered without any hesitation. The smile curving her lips made her partner uneasy. "You owe me a favor."

"Yeah," Francisco said with a resigned sigh. There was no question that she had covered for him a couple of times and probably would do so again in the future. "I'll see what I can do. By the way," Del Campo asked, looking at the clock on the far wall, "isn't Mystery Man supposed to be here by now like the rest of us hardworking peasants? It's almost nine and it's a little early in the game to be slacking off, don't you think?"

She had no idea why she felt this sudden protectiveness going into high gear within her, but there it was.

"Muldare's not slacking off. He's taking care of a personal matter," she informed Del Campo.

Or at least she hoped that was what Jackson was doing, Brianna thought. She'd certainly told him to call his brother enough times yesterday. Maybe he had, and that had led to some sort of an emergency or crisis that he had to take care of.

Francisco seemed really amused as he regarded her. "My, getting kind of defensive on his behalf, aren't you, Bri?" he asked.

"I'm not being defensive," she informed Francisco crisply. "I just don't want you to get the wrong idea about Muldare, so I'm filling you in." It was time to redirect Del Campo's attention back to the case, otherwise he was liable to go on about Muldare indefinitely. "In the meantime, you want to take some of the people on this list and see if they have anything enlightening about the hotel to offer?"

Taking the new list Brianna had printed up just before he'd come in, Francisco looked over the names and the current information beneath each one. Scanning it, he nodded.

"I've always been partial to the beginning of the alphabet," Del Campo said with a touch of sarcasm, "so I'll take this bunch and pay them a visit."

"Why don't you take Johansson with you?" she suggested. When she saw the quizzical look entering Del Campo's eyes, she told him, "Two pairs of ears are better than one."

The other detective snorted. "Not if one of those pairs of ears belongs to Johansson. That guy doesn't stop talking from the second he gets in the car."

"Look at the bright side. Maybe you'll pick up some interesting gossip," she told the detective, referring to his attempt to pick her brain when he'd come in.

Francisco looked far from placated. "His stuff doesn't interest me." And then he looked past Brianna's shoulder toward the squad room doorway. "Well, looks like Prince Charming decided to show up."

Brianna didn't have to turn around to know who the detective was referring to. "Careful, Francisco," she cautioned. "Green is not a good color for you."

Del Campo surprised her by agreeing. "Yeah, you're right," he mumbled. Looking at the list he'd just taken from Brianna, he frowned as he got off her desk. "I'd better go tell Johansson the good news that he's working with us on this case."

"Let me know what you find out," she called after Francisco. And then she turned around just in time to see Jackson sitting down at the desk she'd found for him.

Jackson didn't really want to look her way, but it seemed inevitable. And when he did, their eyes met. Being the new kid on the block, he felt obligated to say, "Sorry, I know I'm late."

"Got a good reason?" Brianna asked.

"Yeah."

The single word was guarded as Jackson braced himself for an onslaught of words and probing questions.

Brianna shrugged. "Okay."

"You're not going to ask me what the good reason is?" he asked, looking at her uncertainly.

"Not if you don't want to tell me," Brianna answered brightly.

Well, he certainly hadn't seen this coming—or not coming, as the case might be. Her reaction just wasn't computing.

"Are you the same person I worked with yesterday?" Jackson asked, tongue in cheek. "The one who kept trying to get me to open up about my business?"

Her curiosity was in high gear, but she had to admit she was enjoying Jackson's confusion.

"You'll find that there are many sides to me," she said with a laugh. "Right now, the side that's being paid to be a homicide detective is front and center. Del Campo got the hotel's former assistant manager to come up with a list of guests who stayed at the hotel over its last year. I spent last night and this morning trying to locate them. Del Campo and Johansson took the first half of the list to interview. We'll take the second."

"Johansson?" Jackson questioned.

"Detective Billy Johansson," she clarified. "Six-year veteran. Two in robbery, four in homicide. Any other questions?"

Jackson had come into the squad room ready to roll. After spending a disheartening forty-five minutes this morning visiting his father and telling the man his name and who he was over and over again, he was ready for anything that would help him take his mind off that soul-crushing scenario. He hadn't been close to his father in any manner of speaking since his teens—when he'd mostly brought an inebriated Ethan home from bars—but seeing the man this way was still taking a toll on him.

In response to her question, Jackson said, "Nope, no other questions. Didn't even want to know that much. Let's get started."

Getting her shoulder bag, Brianna led the way out of the squad room. "You want to drive?"

That was two days in a row that she'd given him the option. He had to admit that he was surprised she did. But maybe she didn't like to drive, Jackson guessed.

Still, he wasn't about to look a gift horse in the mouth. The truth was he didn't trust anyone behind the wheel except for himself.

"Sure."

"Okay, then we'll take your car again," she said as they went down the elevator, taking his silence as agreement.

* * *

Brianna waited until they were in the car and on their way to the first address she had pointed out before she turned to Jackson and finally asked, "So, did you go see your brother this morning?"

Jackson almost laughed. "Well, that didn't take long."

"Did you?" Brianna asked again.

Jackson was beginning to learn that his temporary partner wasn't about to give up until she got what she was after.

"No," he bit off.

"Oh." Maybe admitting that he had actually listened to her advice interfered with some sort of code of ethics, so she tried again. "I thought that since you were late getting in for a second day in a row—"

"I had an emergency to deal with," he answered in a clipped voice. He didn't bother looking her way. "Couldn't be helped."

"Two emergencies in two days," Brianna marveled. "You must lead an exciting life."

"Not hardly," Jackson answered in a monotone. And then, very deliberately, he told her, "My excitement takes place in the field." He blew out a breath. He couldn't have her examining his life under a microscope every time he said something. "Look, if you find my work lacking, you can request to have them send you someone else from major crimes."

She didn't want someone else; she wanted him. He was a good cop—besides, she'd already made up her mind that he was going to be her project.

"And ruin what could be the start of a beautiful friendship?" she asked, miming shock, as she put one hand over what she pretended to be her pounding heart. "I don't think so."

Jackson shook his head. He really didn't know what to make of her. "Did you have to pass a psych exam to join the force?" he asked.

"Yes." The exam was standard procedure in the department's attempt to weed out applicants who were ultimately unstable.

"Maybe someone should review that exam and find a way to make it more stringent," Jackson told her. He knew he was goading her and he was prepared for an explosion.

But he was going to be disappointed again.

"You missed your calling, Muldare," Brianna told him matter-of-factly. "You're rather good at creating diversions."

Stopped at a red light, Jackson looked at her. "Obviously not good enough."

Brianna grinned, pleased with the bantering exchange. "Don't feel bad. I grew up with three brothers. I can see through almost anything."

She wasn't going to give him any peace until he tossed her some sort of bone regarding why he was late this morning. "I went to see my father, okay? Are you happy?"

"Not as happy as your father," she told him with a knowing smile.

Jackson thought of the empty expression in his father's eyes when the latter had looked up at him. "Don't count on that," he said flatly.

"Did you two argue?" she asked sympathetically, guessing that was the reason why Muldare was so stricken beneath his stoic expression.

"I wish." The words had escaped Jackson's lips without his even realizing that he had said anything. But since he *had* said that, Jackson completed the rest of his thought for her benefit. "To argue, he would have had to have been lucid."

For a second, Jackson had lost her. And then suddenly, all the pieces came tumbling together and she realized what he was saying. Muldare had to be talking about his father having dementia.

She didn't have any firsthand experience with the soul-crushing disease, but she knew a number of people who did.

"I am so very sorry," Brianna whispered, placing a light hand on his shoulder.

He shrugged her off, keeping his eyes straight on the road. He didn't want her pity.

"Don't be sorry," he told her icily. "Just stop asking questions."

He was hurting and he didn't even know it, or if he did, he wasn't acknowledging it. But how did she reach him if she couldn't get him to talk to her, Brianna wondered, frustrated. It would come to her. Somewhere along the line, as they worked on this terrible case together, it would come to her.

"That won't be so easy to do if we're trying to interview Mrs. Caulfield or the other people on this list," she told him in an amused tone.

"Damn it, you could infuriate a saint," Jackson bit off.

"And by saint, are you referring to yourself?" she asked innocently.

For some reason, he didn't know why—maybe it was her tone of voice—her question made him laugh. Heartily and for more than just a second. He laughed so hard that it released some of the tension that had been knocking around in his chest.

Taking a deep breath, Jackson pushed aside everything that had eaten away at him this morning and centered himself.

"Okay, let's just focus on this case for now," he told her.

"I was just about to suggest that, Muldare," Brianna responded.

Sure she was, he thought. But for now, peace had broken out between them, and he would take it. He needed that peace in order to concentrate on the case.

They were paying him to be a detective, and right now almost every penny of that money was spoken for. He needed to get his brother clean and his father looked after. Whatever little money was left over, he'd use to take care of himself, but not until his father and his brother were squared away.

There were times when he wondered how he'd got into this kind of position, with all this weight on his shoulders. And there were other times when he just shrugged, accepted his burden and made the best of it. After all, what choice did he have? There was no one else to take care of either his brother or his father and he couldn't turn his back on them, even though there were times—selfish times—when he'd been tempted to.

"You know," Brianna said after a prolonged silence, "you can talk. Or would you rather I asked you another question?"

That did it. His mental funk broke apart and slipped into the background as Jackson started asking her questions about the case and brainstorming with her.

Chapter 10

Roberta Caulfield was a lively seventy-nine-year-old widow with sparkling hazel eyes and short-cropped hair the color of blushing strawberries. Living in the Shadowy Oaks apartments, euphemistically referred to as apartment homes, the petite woman was eager for company and ready to talk about anything the two young people at her door wanted to discuss.

A friendly, trusting woman, the retired third-grade teacher hardly glanced at Jackson and Brianna's credentials when she opened the door a moment after they rang the bell.

Instead, she invited them into her living room,

where she immediately attempted to ply them with lemonade and cookies.

"I just made them. They're fresh out of the oven," she told them proudly. "Please," she said, placing a platter of the chocolate chip cookies on the coffee table. "You'll be saving me from myself. I can't resist them."

Brianna looked at Jackson. She could almost see the words forming in his head. He was going to ask the woman why she bothered baking the cookies if she didn't want to wind up eating them.

For the sake of not antagonizing the woman, she headed him off quickly. "We'd love some," she assured the woman. "They look delicious, Mrs. Caulfield."

"Oh, call me Roberta, please," Mrs. Caulfield insisted, dealing out napkins to both of them. "Johnny, my late husband, called me Bertie, but I always hated that name," she confided. "Still, you can't criticize your husband and tell him what to do, now can you?" The woman chuckled.

Brianna saw a smile curving her partner's mouth. "Some women might," Jackson told the widow, slanting a look in Brianna's direction.

"Mrs. Caulfield—Roberta," Brianna quickly corrected herself, "we'd like to ask you a few questions about the Old Aurora Hotel, if you don't mind."

"Oh, I don't mind at all," Mrs. Caulfield answered. She planted herself on the love seat that faced the sofa they were on. "It was such a lovely establishment," she said with a note of wistful longing in her voice. Reaching for one of her cookies, the woman shook her head as she took a bite. "Such a tragedy."

Listening, Brianna decided to just allow the woman to elaborate on what she meant. Watching Mrs. Caulfield's kindly face, she asked, "Tragedy?"

"Well, yes," the other woman said with feeling. "If it were up to me, I certainly wouldn't have torn down that lovely building. Oh, the memories that were made in that place," she said nostalgically.

"According to the hotel records," Jackson cut in impatiently, "you stayed there on three different occasions before the hotel was closed down."

The woman nodded with enthusiasm. "Yes, that is correct."

Jackson asked the widow what he felt was a logical question. "Why would you stay at the hotel when you were living in Aurora?"

Rather than take offense, to Brianna's relief, Mrs. Caulfield seemed to take the question in stride.

"Well, working my way backward," the woman began, "the first time I stayed at the hotel, it was because my husband surprised me with reservations. He called it a getaway weekend," Mrs. Caulfield recalled, a dreamy smile playing on her lips. "We were celebrating our thirty-fifth anniversary.

"The second time was because Katie, our youngest, was getting married there and she and her fiancé were putting all the out-of-town guests up at the hotel. We stayed there, too. It was a beautiful wedding. I have an album if you'd like to see for yourselves," she volunteered.

"Maybe later," Brianna told the woman. "About the last time…?"

"And the last time…" Mrs. Caulfield's voice trailed off for a moment as she looked at them sadly, tears glistening in her eyes. "The last time was because I'd just lost my Johnny and I wanted to go where we'd had some of our happiest times." Glancing at the plate, she raised her eyes to look at Jackson. "You're not eating, Detective," Mrs. Caulfield pointed out.

"I had one," Jackson replied, trying to sound friendly.

"Oh, one's not enough, dear," the grandmotherly woman chided. "You don't get the full effect of the cookie's flavor until you've had at least two or three more." She pushed the platter closer to him, her meaning clear.

"I'm afraid his limit's one. Detective Muldare can't have too much sugar," Brianna told the woman, coming to her partner's rescue with a solemn expression. "His doctor said sugar isn't good for him."

Mrs. Caulfield was clearly disappointed, but she didn't want to argue. Instead, she nodded. "Can't go against doctor's orders, I suppose," she sighed.

Brianna immediately took advantage of the momentary lull and quickly redirected the woman's attention to the reason they were here.

"Tell me, Roberta, during your stays at the hotel, did you ever observe anything odd or unusual going on? Or maybe something that struck you as odd later, when you looked back on it?" she coaxed.

"Odd?" the older woman repeated, as if she was having trouble comprehending the word. "What do you mean by odd?"

At this rate, they were going to be here all day, Jackson thought. "The workers doing demolition found bodies in the hotel walls," he said bluntly.

Mrs. Caulfield's mouth dropped open. She turned pale as she sucked in air and then covered her mouth to suppress a squeal of alarm.

Brianna shot her partner a really irritated look.

"Well, tiptoeing through the tulips wasn't getting you anywhere," he pointed out.

Brianna looked back at the woman on the love seat. "I'm sorry. I'm afraid that my partner's a little rough around the edges—"

But the former schoolteacher waved away Brianna's words of apology, indicating that they were unnecessary. "Don't apologize, dear. My Johnny was just the same way." She smiled at Jackson. "To tell the truth, you rather remind me of him. He always liked to get to the heart of the matter," she told them with a bittersweet smile. "No beating around the bush for him."

"Well, since the ice has been broken," Brianna

said, "*did* you notice anything unusual during your stays at the hotel?"

"Unusual?" the woman repeated thoughtfully. "The staff was all very nice and the dears were eager to please. Even the last time, when I was there by myself."

She paused again, this time for so long Brianna thought that perhaps she'd drifted off.

Just as Brianna was going to try to get the woman to continue talking, Mrs. Caulfield suddenly told them, "You know, that last time, I thought I heard noises in the walls. You know, some kind of scuffling, the kind of noise made by a really large rodent. I called down to the front desk, but the young man who answered assured me that everything was fine and it was just my imagination."

Mrs. Caulfield leaned forward, lowering her voice like a conspirator sharing secret plans. "But the next morning, when I was checking out of the hotel," she told them, drawing out each word, "I saw an exterminator's truck pulling up."

"And this happened during your third stay?" Brianna asked. Sometimes, she'd found, events seemed to link up in a witness's mind, yielding information that the witness didn't even know they possessed.

"Yes!" Mrs. Caulfield declared excitedly. And then, suddenly, her face clouded over. "Oh, goodness, you don't think—" The woman's hazel eyes widened in complete horror.

There was no way the woman had heard people in the walls, Jackson thought. But she looked so appalled, he felt sorry for her.

"Most likely what you heard *were* rats in the walls," he told Mrs. Caulfield. "They can make a lot of noise and sound like they're everywhere."

Mrs. Caulfield nodded, allowing Jackson to calm her.

"Rats," she echoed. "Yes, you're right. That's probably it," she agreed, her eyes darting back and forth between Jackson and his partner. "That young man at the desk probably didn't want to admit that was the problem. Bad publicity and all that."

"So there's nothing else that you can recall that seemed out of the ordinary?" Brianna asked.

Mrs. Caulfield shook her head. "No, nothing. I even called all the guests who had attended Katie's wedding and asked them if they had a good time. Funny thing, I never got an answer from Tina."

"Tina?" Brianna repeated, wondering if this was just another rambling sidebar the woman was going to launch into.

The strawberry-blond head bobbed up and down. "Tina Rutherford. She was my husband's young cousin. Flirty little thing," Mrs. Caulfield confided nonjudgmentally, then chuckled. "It looked like she and one of the other guests were really connecting. I even tried calling her a second time a couple of days later to find out how that turned out, but she never returned my call," Mrs. Caulfield concluded with a resigned sigh.

"Didn't that concern you or your husband?" Jackson asked.

"Oh, no," Mrs. Caulfield assured him. "Tina was given to taking off on a whim. We just thought that Tina was just being Tina, that's all."

"Did you *ever* hear from her after that?" Brianna asked her.

Mrs. Caulfield thought for a moment. "Come to think of it, no. But then, we weren't close or anything," she explained quickly.

"Did she come to your husband's funeral?" Brianna pressed.

"We couldn't reach her to tell her. Her phone had been disconnected by then," Mrs. Caulfield answered.

Brianna exchanged looks with Jackson. She could see that he appeared to be thinking the same thing: that they had, just possibly, stumbled across the name of one of the victims unearthed by the wrecking ball.

"Roberta," Jackson said in a conversational tone, "we have a few more questions for you."

"Of course, of course," she said quickly, adding, "Anything I can do to help, just name it." Her eyes shifted between them. It was obvious that she could barely contain herself. "This is so exciting—awful," she was quick to add, "but exciting."

Beaming, the older woman pushed the platter of chocolate chip cookies closer to the handsome young detective.

"I think she was actually batting her eyes at me," Jackson said as he and Brianna left the woman's homey little apartment almost forty-five minutes later.

Brianna pretended to consider his observation. "Could have been the sunlight making her squint," she deadpanned.

She expected Jackson to respond curtly, but instead, as they reached his vehicle, he said, "By the way, thanks for the save."

Brianna got in on the passenger side. "Come again?"

"Telling her that I couldn't have too much sugar," he reminded her. "Quick thinking."

She looked at him, stunned. Muldare was actually complimenting her. She was close to speechless for a moment.

"Those had to be the worst cookies I've ever had," he said, starting up his car. As he pulled out, he asked, "How did you eat two of those things?"

Brianna shrugged. "I felt sorry for her, and I have a cast-iron stomach." She paused, thinking about the information they'd managed to glean. "So what do you think? Was Tina Rutherford one of the hotel killer's victims?"

"The hotel killer?" he repeated. "You've labeled him?"

"For now, until something better comes along. So what do you think about Cousin Tina?"

"She could have been a victim," he allowed. "Or maybe she never called back because she just didn't want to risk having to eat any of Mrs. Caulfield's cookies."

Brianna humored him for a second. "A definite possibility." And then she grew serious. "But I'm still going to have Valri in the computer lab see if she can track down this woman from the information that Mrs. Caulfield gave us."

"Meanwhile—" he indicated the list of names that sat on his dashboard "—we've still got all these people to talk to."

Brianna slanted a wicked look in his direction. "Good thing we don't have to do it on an empty stomach," she said.

Jackson groaned. He could swear that his gut was grumbling in protest over the cookie he'd been forced to ingest. "Don't remind me," he said.

The rest of the morning and afternoon were one huge blur as she and Jackson systematically went down the list, interviewing as many of the former hotel guests who currently resided in Aurora as they could.

A number of other guests lived in the outlying cities. Brianna decided that they would get to those people after they'd had the opportunity to talk to the ones who lived in the immediate area.

The guests who now lived out of state would get phone-call interviews. Brianna didn't feel that phone calls were as effective as face-to-face interviews, but for now the phone calls would have to do—unless the phone call caused a red flag to go up.

This, she told Jackson, was the plan for now. He went along with it.

Over the course of that day and the following one, Brianna periodically kept in touch with Del Campo. She wanted to see how he and Johansson were doing and if they'd had any breakthroughs with their interviews.

"Only that I'm seriously beginning to think I need a career change," Del Campo told her the second time she called him.

"That's nothing new," she told him. By her count, Del Campo had a career crisis at least once a month. "How many names are left on your list?"

"Five. Why?" he asked.

His voice sounded like he was really beat to her. A tired detective missed things.

"Look, why don't you and Johansson call it a day and go home?" she told him. "You can get to the last five tomorrow."

"What if that turns out to lead nowhere, too?" Del Campo asked wearily.

"Then we'll get together tomorrow to figure out our next move," she told him matter-of-factly.

It wouldn't be the first time they'd have to re-group and go back to square one, she thought. Only crimes on TV were solved in the scope of sixty minutes minus commercials.

"Hey," she heard Del Campo say, brightening already, "you don't have to twist my arm. Tomorrow," he told her just before ending the call.

"I take it he didn't get anywhere, either," Jackson surmised as Brianna put her cell phone away.

They were on their way back to the precinct. Brianna sighed, leaning back in the passenger seat. She was doing her best not to let frustration get the better of her, but it was a struggle.

"Someone had to have seen or heard *something*," she said, exasperated.

"Trouble is," Jackson speculated, "they probably don't know that they saw it or heard it." That happened far more often than either one of them was happy about. "Why don't you give it a rest tonight, like you told Del Campo to do?" he suggested suddenly. When she turned toward him with a quizzical look, he said, "You look beat."

That was *not* what she wanted to hear. She liked to think of herself as invincible.

"Is that the line you use to have women falling at your feet?" she asked sarcastically.

"No, that's the line I use to get my partner to act sensibly and get some rest," he said without emotion. "I don't want to take a chance on you being so punchy that you don't have my back."

"That'll never happen," she assured him. She didn't like what he was implying.

Jackson didn't back off. "I wouldn't be too sure if I were you."

"You're not me," she informed him tartly just as they pulled into the rear parking lot. "And if you recall, I told Del Campo and Johansson to call it a night. That means that you can, too."

"I wasn't talking about me," he said as they got out of the car.

"Okay," she snapped. "I'll go to bed."

Several police detectives were walking to their cars, and they stopped to look in her direction.

"Alone," she specified to negate what they appeared to be thinking.

"Hey, if you'd like some company," Hardy, a tall blond detective who worked vice, called out, a broad grin on his face, "I'm right here."

"She's not looking for company," Jackson informed the other detective sharply.

"Message received." Hardy gave them a mock salute and disappeared into his vehicle.

Chapter 11

Still standing on the other side of his vehicle, Jackson waited for Brianna to snap at him for feeling as if he had to come to her defense.

Things were a lot easier when acts of chivalry were commonplace and just accepted without being dissected and examined six ways from sundown. These days when he followed his instincts, he was just as likely to wind up insulting someone as he was to do the right thing.

He was still working on squelching those instincts and keeping to himself, but they got away from him at times. Like now. He couldn't explain exactly why, but something about Brianna raised his protective instincts to the surface.

So Jackson had to admit he was rather surprised when Brianna looked at him after Hardy drove off and, instead of telling him she was perfectly able to defend herself, she said, "Thanks."

Recovering, Jackson shrugged in response. "He was being a jerk."

"You'll get no argument from me." Feeling that it would be best to retreat now before it got any more involved, Brianna said, "Well, I'll see you in the morning." She began to walk toward her own car parked a row away.

She'd only taken a single step when she heard Jackson's phone start buzzing. Pausing, she looked over her shoulder in his direction. He was frowning as he stared down at the screen.

"Is that your brother?" she asked.

"Yeah."

That he answered at all surprised Brianna. It also made her feel as if maybe, just maybe, she was making a little headway when it came to burrowing beneath the man's inner shell.

The next minute, he obviously pressed the decline tab, since the phone stopped vibrating.

He couldn't keep doing this indefinitely, Brianna thought. There was a good person under all that. He was just having trouble digging himself out.

"Well, when you do finally decide to go see your brother, if you need any support, I can come with you," she offered.

About to get back into his car, Jackson stopped.

Working on the police force, he was still a loner. He wasn't accustomed to anyone caring enough about him to attempt to help. "Why would you want to do that?"

There was no long, involved response. As far as Brianna was concerned, the answer was simple. "It's all part of having your back—and you having mine," she told Jackson.

"Okay," he finally said. "I'll keep that in mind."

Brianna nodded, getting into her car.

Inch by inch, she thought. She was making progress inch by inch.

Inch by inch, Brianna thought again several days later, but this time she wasn't thinking about her progress in getting Jackson to open up. Instead, she was thinking about the case. Between the four of them, she, Jackson, Del Campo and Johansson had spoken to almost all the guests they could find, except for two, either in person or over the phone. All those man-hours spent and she felt that they were no closer to finding out who was responsible for killing and entombing all the bodies that had been discovered—eighteen so far—than they had been when they'd first started.

The last two former guests on the list had lived in the hotel on a permanent basis. Neither of them was in the area anymore.

At eighty-three, Irene Jessop resided in a retirement home in San Francisco, which was north of

Aurora, while the eighty-nine-year-old Barry Mc-Namara lived with his son and grandson in Napa Valley, where the younger McNamaras operated a vineyard.

"Why don't you take one and we'll take the other?" Del Campo suggested as they gathered around a conference table in the squad room, discussing their next move.

Brianna had been thinking the exact same thing. "Fine with me," she agreed. She turned toward Jackson and asked, "Do you have any preferences as to which of the former permanent guests we interview?"

Jackson appeared to be entirely indifferent. Shrugging, he said, "Up to you."

Del Campo, however, wasn't indifferent. Raising his hand in a mock effort to get Brianna's attention, he told her, "I've always wanted to tour a vineyard."

She had no trouble believing that. Del Campo prided himself on being an expert on different wines.

"You won't be taking a vacation day going up there," she reminded the other man. "This'll be in the line of duty."

"Absolutely," Francisco agreed, then grinned as he added, "but it can feel like a vacation day."

She saw no reason to say no to Del Campo's choice. But in the interests of fairness, she turned toward Jackson again. "Muldare?"

"You're the boss," he told her.

She wasn't buying that. She was the boss until she did or said something that Muldare disagreed with. The man was *not* as easygoing as he was trying to portray. But she'd take what she could get. And saying yes would make Del Campo happy. Happy detectives worked far better and more productively than unhappy ones.

"Fine," she said decisively. "You and Bill go up to Napa and see McNamara," she told Del Campo, who immediately got to his feet. "Muldare and I'll talk to the Jessop woman. Maybe one of them has something we can finally work with," she said. So far, the only so-called "lead" they'd got, the name of the possibly missing wedding guest, Tina Rutherford, hadn't led to anything.

Del Campo and Johansson left the squad room immediately. It was obvious that Del Campo didn't want to take a chance on her changing her mind. Brianna and Jackson were about to leave as well when her cell phone rang.

Heading toward the elevator, Brianna held up one hand and answered her cell with the other. "O'Bannon."

"Detective, I'd like to see you and Detective Muldare in my office."

She didn't have to ask who was calling. Like most of the detectives at the precinct, she could recognize the chief of detectives' voice anywhere. And, just like any other detective at the precinct, she wondered if she'd done anything wrong to prompt this summons.

"Yes, sir. We'll be right there."

Terminating the call after a beat just in case the chief had something more to add, she put her phone back into her pocket.

"Command performance?" Jackson guessed.

She nodded, assuming that Jackson had overheard. "Chief of Ds wants to see us."

The elevator car arrived, and Jackson gestured for her to enter in front of him.

"Age before beauty," he quipped.

"Wrong on both counts," she said, getting into the elevator. She pressed for the floor where the chief of detectives had his office.

"You know," Brianna said, breaking what felt like an endless silence in the elevator as they rode up to the chief of Ds' floor, "most detectives would be speculating as to why the chief of Ds wanted to see them. You, on the other hand, haven't said a word."

"No point in speculating," Jackson answered. He didn't believe in torturing himself with various scenarios. "We'll know why soon enough."

"You are a really strange man," she told Jackson as they reached the seventh floor. "Don't you have *any* curiosity?"

"I do," he admitted mildly. "But I keep it to myself."

Brianna shook her head as she got off. "Really strange," she repeated under her breath.

"He's waiting for you," Lieutenant Laura Rayns told them as they walked into the chief's outer office. "Go right in."

Brianna entered the chief of detectives' very masculine office just ahead of Jackson.

Brian Cavanaugh rose to his feet to greet them.

"Sit, please." When they did and he was behind his desk again, Brian asked, "How's the case coming along?"

Offering excuses had never been the way she operated. She didn't start now. "I'd love to say that we're closing in on the killer, sir, but the truth is, we're not making all that much headway."

Kind, thoughtful green eyes met hers. "No leads?" Brian asked.

"We're following up on a few more things," Brianna answered, hating how very vague that had to sound.

Because the chief of detectives turned to look at him, Jackson joined in. "The medical examiner is still trying to identify the bodies."

"I hear the count is up to eighteen as of this morning," Brian said.

Brianna knew that the man believed in being hands-on when it came to investigations, and he made it a point to be aware of everything that was going on in a case, no matter how many the precinct was juggling.

"Yes, sir, it is," she answered.

Jackson broke it down for the chief. "Fourteen of those victims have been dead around three decades, and four met their deaths far more recently."

"I know," Brian replied. Folding his hands on his desk, he leaned forward slightly. "I also know that there are certain people who are suggesting that we stop wasting precious police resources and drop the case."

This was the first she'd heard of that. "Certain people?" Brianna questioned. "Who?"

Brian smiled. There were detectives under his command who wouldn't think of voicing that question. They merely took orders, obeying to the letter whatever was said. But he preferred having detectives who thought for themselves—he always had.

"The mayor," Brian answered after a long moment had passed. "And certain members of the city council. They're afraid this investigation might offend the Aurora family. And that, in turn, might make the family close its coffers the next time the city finds itself needing extra money—and the city always seems to need extra money."

Brianna stared at the man. His expression was difficult to read. She knew what she *wanted* it to say, but wishing didn't make it so, and she needed to be sure.

"Are you saying you want us to stop the investigation?" Brianna asked.

"I'm saying that if there's any possible way for

you to do this, I want you—" his eyes swept over his niece as well as the detective working with her "—to find out who's responsible for these murders.

"I don't care if most of the crimes *are* over thirty years old. People were deprived of their lives and sealed inside those walls. That kind of thing belongs in an Edgar Allan Poe story, not in my city," he said with passion. "Whatever you need, you'll get. Just find who did this. And if the answer winds up making waves for the Aurora family, well, that can't be helped. I won't have the truth buried in order to spare anyone embarrassment. Have I made myself clear?"

"Perfectly." Brianna and Jackson said the word almost in unison.

Brian smiled, satisfied he'd made his point. "Good," he pronounced. "Now find the killer," he instructed. "Oh," he suddenly remembered just before they reached the door. "One more thing."

Brianna turned back around first; followed a second later by Jackson. They both remained where they were, waiting.

His almost grim look gave way to a far more sunny expression. "It seems that my older brother, Andrew, feels we all need a respite, especially in light of this gruesome case."

Brianna knew what the man seated on the other side of the desk was getting at before he said another word, but because this was his office, and because Jackson was most likely unfamiliar with the social habits of her extended family, she quietly waited for Brian to continue what he was about to say.

"He's having a gathering Saturday, at his place. Everyone's invited, as usual. And if you're unclear about what I am saying, this also means you, Detective Muldare," he told the man standing just behind Brianna. "All right," he told them. "*Now* you can go."

For a moment, Jackson made no comment as they left the chief of Ds' office.

And then, just as Brianna was about to ask him if he'd understood what her uncle had just said, Jackson looked at her, astonished. "He was kidding, right?"

"Which part?" Brianna asked innocently.

"You know damn well which part," Jackson bit off. "The part where I'm supposed to turn up at a so-called gathering." He jabbed the down button with his index finger.

"No, he wasn't kidding about that," she informed Jackson calmly, her tone directly in contrast to his. "He was serious." She paused for a moment, letting her words sink in before she added, "And, since he asked you in person, you really do need to show up."

Jackson didn't like being backed into a corner, especially since there was so much in his life that he wasn't able to control.

"Why?" he asked. "Why would it matter to him one way or another?"

She lifted her shoulders, then let them drop again. "Maybe he feels you need to socialize a little with your fellow cops."

He eyed her suspiciously. "You talked to him about me, didn't you?"

"Nope. Not a word," Brianna answered, elaborately crossing her heart.

"The man's got a hell of a lot of people under his command. How would he even *know* that I need to socialize?"

Brianna spread her hands wide as they got off the elevator.

"He's the chief of Ds. He knows everything." She said it so seriously, for a minute, Jackson found himself almost believing her.

"Then he knows I won't come," Jackson concluded, thinking that was finally the end of it.

One look at Brianna's face as they went outside told him that it wasn't.

"No," she contradicted. "He knows that you will." Brianna told him that with such calm certainty, he could have sworn he heard the jaws of a trap snapping shut around him.

"It's not as bad as you think," Brianna assured him as they continued walking toward his vehicle. "It'll only be for a few hours." She was lying about that, but he didn't need to know. "Think of it as on-the-job training."

About to get into the driver's seat, he stopped to glare at her. "What the hell is *that* supposed to mean? What kind of training?"

She smiled as she got into the car on the other side. "Mingling with your fellow officers and detectives without snarling."

"Aren't these things supposed to be for the family?" he asked. Maybe she was just putting him on about having to show up no matter what.

"Uncle Andrew is the one who initially began having these gatherings years back, right after he took early retirement in order to raise his kids. Before he did that, he was the chief of police. And as the chief of police, he regarded everyone under his command as family. So," she told him as he started the car, "like it or not, you, Detective Jackson Muldare, are family, as far as Andrew Cavanaugh is concerned. And between you and me, the chief of Ds likes to keep his older brother happy. Long story short—"

"It's too late for that," Jackson told her dourly as a dark expression descended over his face.

Brianna didn't pay any attention to him. Instead, she concluded what she was trying to tell him. "Long story short, you're coming to the gathering."

Chapter 12

Jackson was in no mood to be trapped in his car, listening to Brianna go on and on about his so-called mandatory attendance at something he had no desire or intention of attending.

"Do you mind if we table this discussion about going to your uncle's gathering for the duration of this road trip?" he asked crisply.

"Sure," Brianna readily agreed. "It can wait until we get back. I'm easy."

Slanting her a quick look, Jackson murmured more to himself than to his partner, "Well, that answers that question."

She waited for him to elaborate. When he didn't, she finally asked, "What question is that?"

"If your nose grows when you tell a lie," he said matter-of-factly. "It doesn't."

Brianna didn't take any offense. She didn't think of herself as being small-minded or petty. But she did feel that she needed to set him straight.

"I don't lie, Muldare."

Jackson found it hard not to laugh at that. "You're also not easy to get along with."

"I'll refrain from pointing out that that's like the pot calling the kettle black," she informed him. The man was definitely a challenge, but she did enjoy a challenge. "Just get your mind back on the case."

"Gladly." Jackson counted to ten—slowly—in his mind. Then, just as Brianna reached over to turn the radio on in an effort to terminate the almost suffocating silence in the car, he asked, "You really think this woman we're traveling all this way to see is going to be able to tell us anything useful?"

"I don't know," Brianna replied honestly. "I'm hoping she'll say something that might trigger something else. Half of all crimes wind up being solved by accident."

A frown darkened his handsome, chiseled face. "That's not exactly reassuring."

"Oh, but it is," she contradicted, "because accidents happen all the time, and in the end, it really doesn't matter just how you figured something out as long as you did."

He shook his head. She was just spouting a bunch of rhetoric, most likely because the woman liked hearing herself talk. It could be worse. She could have a voice that sounded like nails dragging along a chalkboard.

"Still say this is a wild-goose chase. After all, all the other people we've interviewed in the last few days didn't enlighten us," he reminded her.

She studied his profile. The man could have been chiseled out of granite. "You've always been a pessimist, haven't you?"

He didn't even have to think about his answer. The path he was on had been set years ago. "Pretty much. Although I'm not a pessimist," he corrected. "I'm a realist."

"Reality can be pretty nice at times."

They might both be police detectives, but they came from totally different worlds. Hers was made up of roses, his was the thorns. "Not from my point of view," he answered.

Sympathy filled her. "Hard life right from the beginning?"

All right, he'd been polite enough, Jackson thought. "This is a car, O'Bannon, not some shrink's couch. Stop trying to act like one," he warned sharply.

"I'm not trying to shrink you, Jackson," she protested, because she really *wasn't* trying to do that. "I'm trying to be your friend."

"I don't remember advertising for one," he told her shortly. He caught himself before his temper erupted. "Look, you've got your view of the world, and it seems to be working for you. I'm happy for you, but don't try to tell me that life's all sunshine and roses, because it's not," he said with emphasis. "Not when your mother walks out on you and your old man tries to drown the pain every night in a sea of alcohol while your little brother tries to find his peace in any drug he can get his hands on.

"Damn it," he cursed, angry with her, angrier with himself, "why do you keep pushing like this?" Jackson snapped. He hadn't meant to tell Brianna anything, least of all what he'd just allowed to spill out. But somehow, despite his resolve to keep everything to himself, the words had come pouring out of their own accord.

"Because once it's all out, then you can deal with it. *We* can deal with it," she emphasized.

There was fury in his eyes when he glared at her. "There is no *we*," he told her coldly.

But Brianna had been raised holding her own against three brothers and, on occasion, her sister as well. She wasn't about to back off.

"There are two people in this car," she pointed out very calmly. "Two people form 'we.'"

Jackson blew out a breath, trying his best to hang on to his temper. Trying not to tell Brianna off or curse at her for invading his life like some sort of insidious virus. Most of all, he wanted her to keep her distance from him because the woman was getting to him in ways he was trying very hard to resist. Damn it, why didn't she have the kind of face that stopped clocks instead of his heart?

"Why hasn't anyone strangled you yet?" he asked.

He heard her laugh, as if his comment really amused her. It wasn't meant to. "I'm very fast on my feet."

"I'd keep my running shoes on if I were you."

Brianna nodded. "Duly noted."

He could hear the smile in her voice. The woman really was one of a kind.

Jackson drove faster.

"You've got company, Irene," the tall, muscular aide at the residential senior-care facility said.

Irene Jessop slid her hand primly over the housedress covering her lap, as if pressing the wrinkles with her palm would somehow make her garment— and thus her—more presentable. Looking up through her bifocals, she blinked several times before earnestly asking, "Do I know you?"

Brianna sat down on the bed next to Irene's wheelchair. "We're from Aurora. I'm Detective O'Bannon, and this is Detective Muldare. We'd like to ask you a few questions, if you don't mind."

The woman's eyes brightened. "I remember Aurora," Irene said. "I think I'm from there."

"You are," Brianna told her kindly.

Irene nodded, absorbing the information. Her eyes took on a sparkle as she gazed at Jackson. She appeared far more interested in the tall, good-looking man standing next to the person asking her questions.

She flashed a smile at him. "You want to ask me any questions, honey?"

Brianna knew when to take advantage of a situation. Rising from the bed, she silently gestured for Jackson to take her place. With a resigned expression, he did.

"Of course he does," she told Irene. "Detective Muldare always welcomes a chance to talk to an attractive woman."

Irene preened visibly at the endorsement, although she never took her eyes off Jackson. "What's your name, honey?" she asked Jackson.

"Detective Muldare," he told her, even though Brianna had just identified him.

"No, your *first* name, honey," Irene emphasized, looking for all the world like a cat waiting to pounce.

"It's Jackson, ma'am."

Irene beamed as if he had just shared a precious secret. "Like the president."

"Right," he agreed. "Like the president."

"*You* can ask me anything you want, Jackson," the woman told him, sounding almost breathless as she practically devoured Jackson with her eyes.

Tamping down her amusement, Brianna mouthed, "Go for it," and crossed her fingers that this was going to be the break they were hoping for.

Irene reached over and took Jackson's hand in

hers. For a woman in her eighties, she had a remarkably strong grip.

"I'm waiting, Jackson," Irene coaxed.

Jackson got started.

Irene Jessop talked for close to two hours, giving her visitors the impression that she very possibly could go on talking forever. But as she continued talking, it was becoming painfully apparent that none of what she was telling them was leading to anything substantial.

As the second hour elapsed, Brianna decided that it was time to save her partner and wrap the interview up. The aide had brought her a chair to sit on, and she rose to her feet.

Relieved, Jackson quickly took the cue and did the same. Irene's hand had slackened, so he took the opportunity to free himself of her hold.

Irene appeared distressed. "Oh, but you're not leaving, are you?" Her question was directed at Jackson.

Coming to his rescue, Brianna told the woman, "We've taken enough of your time."

"No, no, you haven't," the woman protested. As she reached for Jackson, he heard the sound of a lawn mower revving up somewhere on the property. Irene jumped, her hand flying over her heart.

The lawn-mower noise made carrying on a normal conversation impossible. About to use the noise as an excuse to leave, Brianna saw the old woman's growing agitation.

Jackson bent over the old woman. "Are you all right?" he asked her.

She seemed clearly distressed as she said to him, "Can't get away from it anywhere, can I?"

"Get away from what?" Jackson asked her. "The noise?"

The woman bobbed her silver-gray head up and down. "Yes, noise. Always noise. Just like at the hotel," she complained.

Brianna and Jackson exchanged looks.

"There was noise at the hotel?" she asked the woman. "What kind of noise?"

"Noise," she insisted, frowning. The memory obviously agitated her. "They were always building, building, building. Just when you thought they were finally finished, they'd start up again. Adding more rooms, putting in more walls."

"Who's 'they'?" Brianna asked.

But Irene appeared oblivious, not hearing the question. Her attention was still focused completely on Jackson.

"Who's the 'they' you're talking about, Irene?" Jackson asked her.

Irene lifted her thin shoulders up and then let them drop in a hapless shrug. "I don't know. People. Builders building."

Jackson tried again. "Did you recognize any of them?" he pressed.

Irene's eyes seemed to lose their focus. "Faces. Lot of faces," she told him, then repeated, "Lot of faces. I finally had to move. A person can't sleep with all that noise going on. Hardly anyone left at the hotel," she told her visitors. "Didn't make sense to keep building. But I couldn't take it. I had to move," she mumbled. "I miss it," she lamented. "Miss the hotel."

And then, midword, the old woman stopped talking and her head fell forward.

Alarmed, Brianna crossed over closer to Irene. Jackson was checking her pulse. "She's not—"

"No, she's not dead," Jackson reassured her. "She's just asleep."

He looked at Irene Jessop thoughtfully. As he gently placed her hand back down, Irene began to snore quietly. Jackson took the throw that was on the end of her bed and spread it out over her lap and shoulders to cover her.

When he saw Brianna watching him, he murmured self-consciously, "Old people get cold faster than we do."

You do have a heart in there, Jackson Muldare, Brianna thought, pleased. It took effort not to grin at him. She knew that would set him off.

"Do you think any of what she told us was real?" he asked as they left the residential facility.

"I do," Brianna told him with conviction, getting into his car. "It's undoubtedly mixed in with things she imagined, but I'm willing to bet that what she said has more than an element of truth in it." She buckled up, her mind whirling as she made plans. "We need to dig into the Old Aurora Hotel's history, find out the names of the contractors who worked on the place, did renovations, things like that. They would have had to file any upgrades they did with the city."

"If they were honest and not working off the books," Jackson pointed out.

She sighed. He was right. "There is that," she agreed.

Jackson switched lanes. "Might not be a bad idea to check out if there were ever any police reports filed about wild parties, people being arrested in or around the hotel," he suggested.

Brianna nodded. "Good point."

"Oh, like you wouldn't have thought of doing that," Jackson said.

She was patronizing him, Jackson thought. Probably to get him to drop his guard—and then she'd pounce, ready to convince him to come to that damn gathering she kept pushing.

"I would have," she readily agreed. "But you thought of it first and saved us some time." He had to be the hardest person to compliment, Brianna thought. He seemed to suspect everything. The man must have had one hell of a crummy childhood, she thought, sympathy stirring in her. She switched subjects. "See, I told you this wasn't going to be a waste of time."

"No, you *hoped* this wasn't going to be a waste of time," he pointed out. "There's a difference."

"Do you have to argue about everything?"

"Do you?" he countered.

She took a deep breath, doing her best to center herself and walk away from any potential dispute that was brewing. "We got a win here, Muldare. Why don't we just run with it for now and see where it leads?"

"Fine with me."

"By the way," she said as Jackson made his way to the freeway on-ramp that would eventually bring them back to Aurora, "how long have you known that you possessed this fatal appeal to women of a certain age?" She was having trouble getting the question out without laughing.

"Let it go, O'Bannon," Jackson retorted. "It got her talking and that led to what you seem to think is a break, so why don't you give *me* one and let this drop?"

This was just the normal give-and-take of a relationship that was formed driving to and from work, but Jackson was obviously not happy having to deal with it, Brianna thought.

"I don't want to let it drop," she told him. "If it wasn't for you, we wouldn't possibly be staring down our first large break. That was good work back there with Mrs. Jessop."

He looked at her while they were stopped at a light. Brianna sounded genuine enough. Maybe she was trying to be friends despite his rebuff earlier.

However, what he'd told her was true. He didn't want friends—all he wanted was some peace and quiet.

Right, peace and quiet. In the middle of a homicide investigation. Boy, did you ever make the wrong career choice, he mocked himself.

"She just wanted to talk to someone," he told Brianna.

"Not someone," Brianna corrected. "You. She wanted to talk to you. Don't forget, I tried to talk to her first. But her eyes didn't light up until she took a closer look at you."

He made a dismissive noise. "Now you're just making things up."

"No," she argued, "I'm just telling it the way it is. Look, young or old, most women respond to a good-looking man. And if that good-looking man is sympathetic, all the better. You use whatever tools you have to get the job done, Jackson. No shame in that."

Most women, he thought. Was she including herself in that? Was she telling him she wanted him to be sympathetic to her? *Let it go, Muldare,* he ordered. *Woman's getting into your brain and creating scenarios there that have nothing to do with the case.*

"I'm not ashamed," he told her. "I just think you're exaggerating."

"On occasion," Brianna agreed. He didn't have to look at her to know she was grinning again. "But not this time. You do own a mirror, don't you?"

"I think there's one in my bathroom," he answered drily.

"Take a look the next time you're in there," she advised. "You'll see what I'm talking about."

"Uh-huh."

Before she could say anything further, Jackson turned on the radio. Loud.

Chapter 13

"Feel like grabbing a pizza or something?" Brianna asked once they were finally back in Aurora and driving toward the precinct.

Traffic from San Francisco had been unusually heavy, and what should have been less than an hour's drive home had turned into a bumper-to-bumper affair that had lasted close to two and a half.

"Pizza sounds good," Jackson answered. Making a sharp right turn at the corner, he glanced at the dashboard. It was after seven. "But I've got somewhere else I'm supposed to be," he told her. Ordinarily, he would have stopped there. But something egged him on to add, "Maybe next time."

Damn it, he was getting soft, Jackson thought, immediately regretting the addendum.

"Need company?" Brianna asked as he pulled into the precinct's parking lot.

"No," he answered flatly, irritated. "You can't just go inviting yourself along," he told Brianna, turning off the car's engine. He knew what had prompted her offer. Somehow, she'd sensed where he was going—or thought she had.

Well, he wasn't about to admit to that. Instead, he tried to throw her off. "What if I was meeting someone?" he questioned, then for emphasis added, "What if I was meeting a woman?"

Her smile told him he wasn't fooling her.

"You would have led with that. Besides," she said, unfazed, "you've kind of established that you don't have a social life."

"When?" Jackson asked, stunned. "When did I establish that?"

Brianna's smile was mysterious as she slid out of the passenger seat. Turning to close the door, she leaned in through the open window and said, "You're a detective, Muldare. Think about it. It'll come to you," she said easily. "See you in the morning."

They weren't parting company just yet, Jackson thought, beginning to get out on his side.

"Where are you going?" Brianna asked.

He jerked his thumb toward the precinct. "I've got to sign out."

But Brianna shook her head, stopping him before he had both feet on the ground. "Don't worry about it. I'll sign out for you. I need to check on something before I call it a night."

She waited a beat for Jackson to ask her what she was checking on, but he didn't. Sitting back down in the driver's seat, Jackson just started up his car again and drove out of the parking lot without so much as a backward glance.

Brianna laughed softly to herself. "Better man than I, Gunga Din," she murmured under her breath.

If the tables had been turned, her own curiosity would have urged her to ask Jackson what he was checking on in the squad room. But he was obviously content not knowing.

How the hell did that man ever make it to detective, Brianna wondered. Curiosity was supposed to be a natural component in the makeup of a police detective, yet he didn't seem to possess it, at least not outside of work-related topics.

Shaking her head, Brianna got on the elevator and pressed the button for the fifth floor.

The squad room was mostly empty when she walked in. The detectives who usually populated the room, unless they were actively on call, had gone home for the night.

Del Campo's desk was vacant, as was Johansson's. The two detectives either hadn't made it back from their wine-country excursion or they had wrapped up the interview and gone straight home. Knowing Del Campo, she mused, they were probably still there, although *not* still interviewing the former hotel resident.

Since she hadn't received any calls on her cell phone, Brianna checked the phone on her desk for messages. The light on it was blinking. The first message turned out to be from Del Campo.

"Best interview you've ever sent me out on, Bri," she heard him say enthusiastically. "The old guy rambled a lot and he wasn't all there, so the interview wasn't really productive, but damn, this really is pretty country. I know where I want to live when I retire. Check in with you in the morning."

The second call, surprisingly, was from Andrew Cavanaugh. The former chief of police didn't usually call her directly.

"Don't know if you've heard by now, but the family hasn't gotten together for over a month, and I feel it's about time. Brian tells me that you've been working a rather tough case, which means that you and your team could use a break for a few hours. I'm having a gathering at my place Saturday. Nothing fancy, just the usual. Good food, good company. Usual time, too, but you can come earlier if you want. Door's always open."

Brianna smiled as the message ended. She supposed that far more urbane, sophisticated people would probably laugh at her, but there was something immensely reassuring and comforting about that deep, warm voice extending an invitation and telling her something that she had heard many times before—that she was welcome.

This was something, she was fairly certain, that Jackson never had in his life. She really wished that the solemn detective would let her in. She was positive that if she could get him to open up, he would wind up feeling better overall.

She came to attention as the phone clicked and launched into the third message. She recognized that voice, too, but without the same warm reaction she'd had to Andrew's.

"Detective, this is Winston Aurora. Sorry to bother you, but I was just wondering how you were doing with the case. Every morning I find myself perspiring as I wait for the story to break on the local news. So far it hasn't, and I thank you for that. None of us in the family wants to deal with intrusive reporters asking nonsensical questions. I do want to remind you of your promise to call me the moment you find any information about the killer. I'm interested in justice being done as much as you are. Thank you for all your fine work and your consideration. Again, please call me. Night or day."

"'Interested in justice being done.' Now, there's a phrase to hang up on your wall. Just what are you so antsy about, Mr. Aurora?" she asked as the machine clicked again, this time shutting off after the last new message. "You know more than you're telling, don't you? But what is it that you know, and how do I get you to tell me?"

Nothing but silence greeted her words, and nothing came to mind. Brianna decided that she was just too tired tonight to deal with an intricate mental puzzle. Tackling something like that required her being rested and sharp. Right now she felt totally dull and incapable of putting two and two together, much less finding the common link between the old and new murders.

Tomorrow, she told herself. She would approach all this from a fresh angle tomorrow.

After all, she reasoned, the victims wouldn't be any deader tomorrow than they were now.

She took what she needed from her desk and locked up for the night. Going home and getting some rest were sounding pretty good to her right about now, Brianna thought.

But first, she had two more stops to make before she could make home—and bed—a reality.

"How are you doing, Jimmy?" Jackson asked, walking into his young brother's small, utilitarian room at the rehab center. Jimmy was sitting in the room's lone chair, reading a worn paperback collection of Mark Twain's short stories, a book he'd read more than once as a kid.

Surprise registered on Jimmy's gaunt face. The smile that instantly rose to his lips disappeared after a beat, replaced by a look of annoyance.

"You haven't been returning any of my calls," Jimmy accused.

"I'm working a new case," Jackson explained. "And you need to feel like you can stand up on your own two feet when I'm not around. I can't always be around," Jackson emphasized.

"You're my brother," Jimmy cried, his emotions getting the better of him. "I'm supposed to be able to count on you."

"I am and you can," Jackson told him calmly. "But more, you're supposed to be able to count on yourself."

"Yeah, right," Jimmy answered sarcastically. "How can I?" he demanded the next moment. "I'm a product of the old man and *her*."

Jimmy hadn't used the word *Mom* since she had walked out on them.

"So am I," Jackson responded quietly. "So am I."

Jimmy looked at him as if this was a revelation, and from the expression on his face, in a way, it was. Wrapped up in self-pity, it was something Jimmy had never quite considered before. "You are, huh?" he repeated like a man who had stumbled across something that could very well unlock the secret of life—or at least give him the key that would help him try to work the lock.

"I am," Jackson said in the same quiet voice, putting his hand over his brother's, silently recognizing and strengthening the bond between them.

Jackson wasn't prepared for his brother to start crying. The sight of tears made him uncomfortable and left him feeling as if there was something lacking inside him—compassion, perhaps. The truth was that he usually had no idea what to do or say in this sort of a situation.

This time, however, even though he still didn't give voice to any sentiments, some sort of protective instinct kicked in. Without a word, Jackson took his sobbing brother into his arms and just held him.

He held Jimmy like that for a long time, until his brother's tears and sobs finally receded.

No two ways about it, Jackson thought. He felt completely wiped out when he pulled into his designated parking spot at his apartment.

The scene at the rehab center with Jimmy had turned out to be cathartic for both of them. Certainly for Jimmy, but he was surprised that it had affected him, too. For the first time in he didn't know how long, Jackson felt something toward his brother other than frustrated anger.

Maybe being around Brianna was rubbing off.

Not that he was about to say anything of the sort to her, he thought the next moment. The woman was bossy enough as it was. If he attributed something positive to her constant harping and preaching, he'd never hear the end of it.

No, this was something that he definitely intended to keep to himself, Jackson silently promised himself.

Turning off the engine, Jackson sat in his car for

another moment or so, allowing himself to dwell, just a little, on the good feeling he was experiencing.

Exhaustion, however, was diminishing that good feeling's aura. As was hunger. His stomach was making all sorts of strange noises at this point. Jackson tried to remember if there was anything even vaguely edible in his pantry or his refrigerator.

The only thing that came to mind was a box of cereal he'd opened more than a month ago. The cereal turned out not to be to his liking, but he hadn't got around to throwing it out yet. And it had to be really stale by now.

Still, he thought as he got out and locked his car, if stale cereal was the only thing he had to eat in the house, he would have to make do. After all, the flakes weren't poisonous—as far as he knew.

As he drew closer to his ground-floor garden apartment, he saw something on the ground right in front of his door.

A flat square box.

Jackson frowned.

Any packages that didn't fit in the mailbox were left in the complex manager's office. Packages were definitely *not* left on an apartment doorstep.

Suspicious, Jackson looked around to see if there was any sign of someone watching him, waiting for him to pick up the box or at least examine it.

There was no one.

He took a step closer to the box. The breeze shifted, and that was when he smelled it.

The very strong, tempting aroma of freshly baked pizza was coming from the box.

The tantalizing aroma went along with the logo printed on the box.

Mario's Pizza.

Jackson carefully looked around again for whoever had left the box.

Still nobody.

He crouched down and saw a small piece of paper tucked into one side of the box. Carefully taking it out so he didn't rip it, Jackson unfolded the paper.

Knew you'd forget to stop to get dinner. Thought you might be really hungry by now. This is my favorite—pizza with everything. Enjoy! O'Bannon. PS How did your visit with your brother go?

Stunned, Jackson sat back on his heels, staring at the note. Damn, this was positively eerie, he thought. On two counts.

How did O'Bannon know where he lived?

And how the hell did she know he had gone to see his brother? He hadn't been a hundred percent sure that he was going to the rehab facility until he'd actually got out of the car there. Halfway there, he'd almost changed his mind and turned his car around to go home.

"This proves it," Jackson muttered under his

breath. "The woman's a witch, pure and simple."
Holding on to the pizza box, he rose to his feet.
"There's no other explanation for it."

The smell of the pizza was making him sali-
vate, and the box still felt hot. What had she done,
raced over with it?

Why?

What made her do something like that? It wasn't
as if they were actual friends. They weren't even
close. He'd purposely tried to squelch her attempts
to get closer to him, or to share any sort of personal thoughts.

What did it take to make the woman take a hint
and finally back off?

Obviously he hadn't stumbled across the secret
to that because if this pizza was any indication,
O'Bannon was coming full steam ahead.

Look on the bright side, Jackson thought. *At
least you have dinner.*

And then, as he let himself into his apartment,
what he had just thought hit him with the force of
a charging rhino.

He'd just told himself to look on the bright side.

Damn, Jackson thought as he put the pizza box
down on the small kitchen counter. The woman
actually *was* rubbing off on him.

He hadn't been capable of looking on the bright
side of anything for many, many years.

Not until now.

Chapter 14

Brianna was at her desk in the squad room early the next morning, researching the Old Aurora Hotel's history. She was there earlier than usual because she had a feeling that Jackson would turn up early as well. She had no doubt that Jackson probably wanted to talk to her, and anything he had to say to her she wanted as few people to overhear as possible. When he got worked up, his voice tended to carry.

She absently took a sip of the coffee she'd picked up on her way in, her eyes on the screen. The coffee was already getting cold. Frowning, she put the cup down.

Brianna was only beginning to delve into the

history of the work permits taken out for the Aurora Hotel when Jackson arrived.

Rather than going to the desk he was assigned to, he came directly to hers. She felt Jackson's presence before he even said a single word and braced herself.

"How do you know where I live?" he asked, fairly growling out the question. He'd spent half the night expecting Brianna to pop up on his doorstep with some sort of dessert.

Brianna looked up at him, her eyes deliberately wide and innocent.

"What, no 'hello'? No 'how are you'? No 'the pizza was good'?" she asked.

"Hello, how are you, the pizza was good," Jackson parroted. "How the hell do you know where I live?"

"I'm a detective," she told him cheerfully. "I detect."

"*Why* did you detect where I live?"

There was no reason for her to have sought him out and left a freshly prepared pizza on his doorstep. They were working on a case together—most likely for only a short term. They meant nothing to each other.

"Well," she answered, sounding serious, "after I picked up the pizza, I couldn't very well go driving up and down the streets of Aurora, shouting, 'Pizza delivery for Jackson Muldare. Come out, come out wherever you are, Muldare.'"

Jackson bit back a number of choice words. The woman won the prize—she was officially the most frustrating person he had ever tried to carry on a conversation with.

"That's not the point," Jackson insisted, struggling not to shout.

As far as Brianna was concerned, she had done a nice thing and he was biting off her head. She was in no mood for his temper tantrum.

"No," she said, measuring out each word, "the point is I dropped off dinner for you and you come in this morning acting like a wounded bear."

"I didn't ask you to drop off dinner," Jackson retorted.

She took a breath, counting to ten. She *wasn't* going to lose her temper. "I didn't say you *asked* me to do it. I did it because I figured you were hungry and sometimes it's nice coming home to a warm meal."

"I don't need coddling—"

Okay, that did it. Being nice to this man definitely wasn't working. "No, you need to be hit upside the head and taught manners and I'd love to be the one to do it, but hey, we all can't have what we want," she snapped, raising her voice in order to get through his thick head.

"Anything wrong out here?" Lieutenant Eric Hendricks came out of his small office to investigate the shouting.

Brianna tamped down her temper. "No, nothing's

wrong, Lieu. Muldare and I were just having a difference of opinion on how to proceed with the case."

Rather than retreating to his office the way Brianna had hoped, the newly appointed lieutenant crossed to her desk. "And just how *are* you proceeding with the case?" he asked. "Winston Aurora called me last night asking questions about the department's progress. I told him I'd get back to him. Give me something to get back to him with."

She nodded. "He left a message on my landline asking the same thing while Muldare and I were out, questioning one of the hotel's live-in residents."

"And?" he asked.

"We're checking out a few things," Jackson said. When the lieutenant raised a quizzical eyebrow in his direction, Jackson elaborated, "Like the names of the various contractors involved in renovations on the hotel at different points in time. Lots of ways those bodies could have gotten into the walls."

Listening, the lieutenant nodded solemnly. "I just hope none of those ways involved anyone from the Aurora family. Not that I like any of those snobs, but they can make life hell for the department if they think one of their own is under suspicion," he told the two detectives. "Okay, carry on. Just not so loudly."

"Yes, sir," Brianna answered.

"Sorry. My fault," Jackson told the lieutenant.

Hendricks nodded. "Nothing wrong with having a passion for your work, I guess," he responded just before he closed the door again.

Once the lieutenant had returned to his office, Brianna turned toward the major crimes detective. "Why did you just lie to the lieutenant? I was expecting you to feed me to the wolves."

Jackson shrugged carelessly. "Not my style. Besides, I didn't lie. Everything I said we were doing we discussed last night on the way back from San Francisco." Just about to cross over to the desk he was currently occupying, he paused to look at Brianna over his shoulder. He felt himself softening. Again. This had to stop. He had to put a stop to having these feelings about her that popped out of nowhere. "And the pizza *was* good," he told her grudgingly.

Brianna smiled, pleased. "Good," she echoed just before she got back to work.

"Man," Del Campo declared, walking into the squad room some thirty minutes later, "I wish all our suspects were out in wine country."

"Mr. McNamara wasn't a suspect," Brianna pointed out to the other detective. "He was supposed to be a possible witness."

"Not in his present condition, he wasn't," Del Campo told her. "The guy couldn't tell cartoons apart from regular people."

Del Campo had completely lost her. "Come again?" Brianna asked.

Johansson was walking in right behind Del Campo. "The old guy was watching some cartoon movie when we came to see him," he explained. "He kept getting confused when he saw the commercial breaks, thought the actors were chasing away the cartoon characters. That's when he started narrating, trying to make us understand what was happening." Johansson shook his head. "Because he thought we weren't following what was going on."

"Yeah," Del Campo recalled. "There was this old guy and this young girl in the cartoon. McNamara kept telling us what was going to happen next." Del Campo frowned, shaking his head. "For an old man, McNamara had one hell of a grim imagination." He underscored his statement with an exaggerated shiver. "That part really sucked," he murmured before he finally walked off to his desk.

But Brianna's interest had been piqued. "Why?" she asked, following Del Campo. "What did he say?"

Del Campo shrugged. "Just all sorts of weird stuff. McNamara was telling the girl—she was a squirrel, by the way," he interjected with an incredulous laugh. "He was yelling at the TV, telling her to be careful. That the old guy—a polar bear, by the way—was going to make her disappear. Bury her inside a block of ice. Just weird stuff," he reiterated.

"Did you try to get him to talk about what made him say that?" Brianna pressed.

Maybe McNamara was reliving something he might have witnessed going on at the hotel, she thought. Brianna was aware that she was grasping at straws—but sometimes straws turned out to be a lot more durable than first imagined.

"No," Del Campo answered. "Because that was about the time McNamara got this really blank stare on his face, like he wasn't there anymore." He must have realized that Brianna was taking this seriously. "Hey, Bri, this was all just in the guy's head."

"Yes, but maybe some of it got in his head because of something else," Jackson suggested.

Johansson made a face as he shook his head. "That's reaching. You should have seen him. The guy was three sandwiches short of a picnic."

Brianna didn't doubt it. It sounded like McNamara had dementia—but even dementia patients had their lucid moments. As the other two detectives went over to their desks, Jackson remained standing next to hers. He had a knowing look on his face.

"You're thinking of going to see him, aren't you?"

She didn't have to ask who Jackson was referring to. "Wouldn't be a bad idea. If we don't find anything else to go with," she qualified. "Right now, we have at least three construction companies and subcontractors to look into. I want to find out just what sort of services these companies rendered."

Jackson gave voice to what was obviously on both their minds. "You think one of these companies' contractors sealed those bodies into the wall?"

"Well, they didn't get there by themselves," she pointed out. "And unless the killer was also a contractor, someone had to seal the victims into the walls and do it well enough not to have those bodies detected all these years."

Jackson pointed out, "You're forgetting one thing."

Offhand, she couldn't think of anything, but she was willing to listen. "Which is?"

"Some of those bodies are not as old as the others," he reminded her.

That opened up the possibility of more than one killer—certainly more than one person sealing those bodies into the walls. "Oh damn," Brianna exclaimed. "I did forget."

Jackson snapped his fingers. "And just when I was thinking you were perfect," he said, doing his best to keep a straight face.

"That'll be the day," she laughed drily.

Her eyes sparkled when she laughed, he noticed. There was something almost compelling about the way that looked. Annoyed by that thought, he shifted his attention.

"Well," he said, "maybe close to perfect."

Brianna couldn't help noticing the way Jackson had almost sounded sincere.

She knew he wasn't, but still… *Knock it off, Bri. It's too early in the day for fantasies, and you've got a killer—or killers—to catch. Killers with their own contractor in tow*, Brianna thought sarcastically, momentarily feeling overwhelmed.

Doing her best to rally, she decided to drop by the morgue.

"I'm going to see Kristin to find out if she has a final body count yet," she told Jackson as she rose to her feet. She made a split-second judgment call. "Want to come along?"

Rather than say yes or no, Jackson thought about it. "The morgue, huh?" he asked.

"That's where the bodies are," she told him flippantly.

Jackson never liked being stuck behind his desk. He preferred being out in the field, even if that field, in this case, turned out to be the morgue.

"Sure. Why not?" Jackson answered. "I guess I can't say you never take me anywhere," he quipped.

Bemused, she walked out of the squad room with him.

"Are you forgetting yesterday?" she questioned. "The road trip? Mrs. Jessop?"

There was a long pause before he responded by saying, "I never forget a thing."

She had no idea why, but the expression on his

face made her feel as if he was putting her on some sort of notice.

Again she told herself that her pace was getting to her. She had to stop reading into things. Jackson was just talking to hear himself talk. He didn't mean anything by what he said.

So why say it? Brianna questioned.

She hadn't a clue.

When they walked into the morgue, which was located in the basement of the building across the street from the precinct, there was music playing softly. Rather than something somber, or the classical music one of the other medical examiners enjoyed when he was on duty, Kristin Alberghetti-Cavanaugh had classic rock on the sound system, just loud enough to keep the somber thoughts surrounding the business at hand at arm's length.

There were only two gurneys out today, unlike the last time she and Jackson had visited the morgue. Kristin was working on a body on one gurney while an assistant made written notations about the other.

Also unlike the first time, when all the gurneys had held fragments of bones, the bodies currently awaiting autopsies still had flesh on them, still bore striking resemblances to actual people rather than disintegrating cadavers.

"More bodies from the hotel?" Brianna asked.

"As far as I know, these are the last of them," Kristin replied. "The CSI team has gone through everything in that building and says there are no more bodies to be found in the debris."

"No more in the walls?" Jackson questioned.

"No more walls," Kristin replied. "And no more bodies anywhere else on the hotel grounds."

"So what's the final tally?" Brianna asked, even as she shook her head at the sound of her own words. She almost shivered. "Is it just me, or does that sound really gruesome?"

"It sounds gruesome, all right," Kristin agreed. "But someone has to speak for the dead." She had taken this job, rather than working in a hospital the way her mother had wanted her to, because she saw herself as an advocate for those who no longer could speak for themselves. "And this is the only way that's going to happen.

"And," Kristin continued, "to answer your first question, there were nineteen bodies in total. Fourteen people were murdered sometime between thirty-five and fifty years ago." She frowned slightly, looking down at the body she was about to autopsy. "Five were killed within the last year or so. The one I did before this one met her death about six months ago."

"Her death," Jackson repeated, looking at the medical examiner with piqued interest. "By any chance, are they all—?"

"Female?" Kristin guessed. "Yes." Pausing, she turned toward the two of them, giving them her full attention. "As near as I can tell, the fourteen were killed by someone fairly strong. When we finally put all the pieces together, I found that all the necks had been snapped."

"And the other five?" Brianna asked.

"They were strangled."

"But not by the same person who killed the other fourteen," Brianna guessed.

"It's highly doubtful," Kristin answered. "It's fifty years from the first murder to the last one. Even if it's the same killer, he's not as young or as strong as he once was."

"So we are looking for two killers," Jackson concluded.

Kristin lowered her visor. "That would be my guess."

Chapter 15

The construction company that had originally built the Old Aurora Hotel was no longer in business and hadn't been for at least a decade. However, Brianna discovered, the three companies that were on record for building additions on the initial hotel and making subsequent renovations were still around and doing business.

Or, at least, Brianna and Jackson found, *versions* of the original three companies were still around. As it turned out, all the present owners were out in the field, working.

Pulling together what information they could on the companies, Brianna and Jackson lost no time getting to all three.

First up was Matthews & Son, a company that'd had at least three changes of address since the initial owner had first been contracted to add on to the original Old Aurora Hotel, nearly doubling it in size.

A call to the number on the website sent the detectives to a construction site. Parking as close as they could, they made their way over newly graded ground to John Matthews, a genial, athletic blond man who looked as if he could carry two-by-fours on his shoulders without any effort whatsoever.

"Actually," Matthews said after introductions had been made and Brianna explained why they were there, "I wasn't part of the company when the additions to the Old Aurora Hotel were made." He laughed almost apologetically. "I wasn't even born. My dad and granddad ran the business back then. Granddad was the original Matthews on the logo. Dad was the and Son," Matthews told them with a touch of pride.

"Did either one of them ever talk about working on the hotel, or have any stories they like to tell?" Brianna asked.

Pausing, Matthews thought for a moment, then shook his head. "No. Only thing my dad ever said was that old George was a hard taskmaster and that he tried to stiff him and Granddad every chance he got. He also made a point of overseeing the work, even insisting on doing some of it. Supposedly old George got his start in construction before he ever moved out here. I got the feeling my dad didn't much like the man, and my dad could get along with the devil himself if he had to."

"Are you talking about George Aurora?" Jackson asked the contractor, just to be sure.

"Yeah. According to Dad, the old hotel was George Aurora's baby. He had it modeled after some Southern mansion he lusted after, growing up dirt-poor in North Carolina."

"Anything else you can tell us?" Brianna pressed.

Because it seemed important, Matthews did his best to recall. "If I remember right, my dad said that the old man was never satisfied. Every so often Aurora wanted another wing added on. Which meant more rooms. Not all at once, mind you," he told them. "But every so often, in waves. I think if George Aurora hadn't finally died, that hotel would be as big as half the city by now."

"Has your company done any work on the hotel since you took over?" Jackson asked.

Matthews shook his head. "The Aurora family never called. And if they had," Matthews went on to confide, "I would have turned them down. I hear that the grandsons take after the old man. Who needs to work with fussy prima donnas?" the contractor asked. "Not me. The city's always coming up with a whole bunch of new rules and regulations for contractors. Those are hard enough to deal with without working for the likes of the Aurora family."

Brianna and Jackson asked a few more questions, but that seemed to be the extent of the information Matthews could provide.

Thanking him, they went in search of the second construction company on the list.

The owner of Laurence & Suarez Builders Inc. took some tracking down. They finally found him working just outside the city, rebuilding a house from the ground up. The previous house that had been there had been completely gutted down to the foundation slab.

JD Laurence was shouting orders at his men. The wiry man was apparently one of those bosses who tried to be everywhere at once.

Several attempts to get the man's attention failed. Taking out his badge and identification, Jackson took the lead, practically getting into Laurence's face before the contractor stopped long enough to listen to him and Brianna.

But before anything could be asked, Laurence snapped, "I've got permits for everything." He spared Jackson only one quick glance. "And if I fall behind, I'm going to wind up having to pay a penalty. I've got no time to chitchat. Whatever you want to talk about, call my assistant. Jenny'll answer all your questions for you."

Moving around Jackson, Laurence shouted out an order to one of his crew. Jackson raised his voice. "It's about the work you did on the Old Aurora Hotel," he told the contractor.

That caught the gruff man's attention.

As he turned around, Laurence's eyes were blazing. He was apparently prepared for a fight.

"Everything was done according to spec. There was no pleasing those people. I even cut my fee for the work that was already done just to get out of the contract." Frowning, he made his case. "I hear they went with Samuel Brothers. Good riddance, if you ask me." Unable to resist getting in a final lob, the balding contractor said, "There was just something really off about those people."

This was what Brianna was looking for. "What do you mean by 'off'?" she asked.

Now that they had him going, the contractor temporarily turned his attention away from his current project. He didn't need to think. Apparently, memories of that job were still very vivid in his mind.

"The guy almost had a heart attack when I suggested tearing down some walls to make room for the extension he was proposing." JD Laurence snorted. "Said not to touch the walls, just to add on. I didn't want my company's name on something that slapdash and told him so. He said that as long as he was paying me, he got to call all the shots."

"And by he," Jackson said, "you mean—"

"Aurora," Laurence answered impatiently, as if

the two detectives should have known whom he was referring to.

"George?" Brianna asked. She assumed that it was, but she wanted to be sure.

The contractor shook his head. "No, the other one," he told them.

"Winston?" Jackson asked. When Laurence shook his head again, Jackson supplied another one of the Aurora brothers. "Miles?"

"No," Laurence answered, impatience brimming in his voice.

"Are you talking about Evanston?" Brianna asked the contractor.

"No." This time, Laurence practically shouted the word at them.

Brianna could see that Jackson was annoyed by the contractor's attitude. Any second, this might go badly, and right now they needed the man's cooperation. She put a hand on Jackson's arm, silently restraining him as she asked Laurence, "Then who are you talking about?"

"The kid," Laurence insisted. "Look, I've got to get back to this," he told them. He was already crossing back to the center of what would eventually turn into the first floor of the house. Currently there were sections of freshly poured concrete waiting for load-bearing beams to be inserted.

"Kid," Brianna echoed, trying to remember names of the people populating the Auroras' family tree. "Are you talking about Damien Aurora?"

Laurence turned around again. "Yeah, that's it. Damien. Like the devil in that old movie," he recalled. That settled, the contractor got back to work. His body language told them that he felt he'd wasted enough time on them. "You got any other questions, call Jenny. Like I said, she'll answer them," he said, tossing the words over his shoulder.

"Thanks for your help," Brianna called to the man as she and Jackson went back to his car.

Busy, the contractor appeared not to hear them.

Jackson got in behind the steering wheel, and rather than turn the key in the ignition, he sat for a moment, staring out through the windshield at the construction crew moving swiftly about, focused on strategically sinking load-bearing beams in freshly poured concrete.

"What are you thinking?" Brianna asked. She knew that the beams weren't what had got his attention. She had a feeling that it was probably the exact same thing she was thinking.

Turning to her, Jackson commented, "Looks like we might have another piece on the chessboard we hadn't considered."

"Damien." Up until now, the youngest Aurora family member hadn't even been thought to be involved in this in any way.

"Damien," Jackson echoed, almost to himself.

Brianna blew out a breath. This was getting more and more involved. "Let's go see if anyone at Samuel Brothers has anything to add to this tale of horror."

Jackson frowned, thinking. "There's only one thing we're missing so far."

In her opinion, there was a lot they were missing, but she gamely asked, "What's that?"

"Proof."

Well, there was that, too, she thought. But they were making progress, and she was hopeful about the eventual outcome. "We'll get it."

"That's right," Jackson recalled, putting the car in Drive. "You're the optimist."

Brianna grinned. "I'll win you over yet," she told him.

"Don't hold your breath," he warned.

Jacob Samuels and his crew were all at a work site, working at a development that was going up just south of Aurora.

Because there were various contractors on the premises, all putting up different models within the new development, it took a bit of doing before Brianna and Jackson finally located the owner of Samuel Brothers Construction Inc., Jacob Samuels, who looked like he had never met a bottle of beer he didn't like. Despite having an impressive belly and being in his early fifties, Samuels moved about the construction site like a man half his age.

Showing Samuels their badges and IDs, Brianna told him, "We just need to talk to you for a few minutes, Mr. Samuels." She and Jackson had to do a lot of moving around to keep up with the man, who didn't appear willing to slow his pace.

"If I wanted to talk, I would have been a lawyer. I'm busy," he replied. Moving around them as if they didn't exist, he made a beeline toward one of his men.

"It's about the Old Aurora Hotel," Jackson said to the back of the man's head.

Like the two other contractors, Samuels stopped moving for a moment when he heard the hotel's name.

And then he said, "Hotel's gone. It's been demolished."

At least he stayed abreast of the news, Brianna thought. "But you did work on it back in the day," she said.

Shrugging his shoulders, Samuels tried to sound indifferent. "If you say so. I've done a lot of work on a lot of places."

Jackson had one last salvo and he delivered it. "JD Laurence said that he gave you the referral, turned the job over to you."

Samuels stiffened. "I did my penance," he said, turning around to look at them. "What about it?"

"You remember anything about that project?" Jackson asked.

"Like what?" Samuels asked suspiciously.

"Like anything unusual or odd?" Brianna supplied. Holding her breath, she watched his face for any telltale signs.

Samuels shrugged again. But the look of indifference was forced now. "The pool out back was cracked in several places. The kid wanted me to fix it, but he didn't want us to jackhammer out the old cement. He insisted that my men patch the cracks and pour fresh concrete over it. I told him the job wouldn't be as good, but he didn't care. Said he didn't want to disturb the hotel guests with all that noise. Like he really cared about disturbing them," Samuels mocked. "He wasn't exactly the thoughtful type. But hey, he paid top dollar. I made sure he knew the risk he was running—that it would have to be done again because that repaving wasn't going to last as long as doing it from scratch. He said that was the way he wanted it, so that's what we did."

Brianna was watching the contractor intently. "And that's it?"

"That's it," Samuels told them.

"Thanks for your time," Brianna told him.

"Hey, wait," he called out to them. "Now that I think about it, there was this one thing. If you could call it that," he said, backtracking.

Jackson and Brianna exchanged looks. "Go on," Jackson said.

"Might just be this kid's imagination," Samuels qualified.

Brianna could feel herself growing impatient. "What kid? Damien?"

"No," Samuels demurred. "I'm talking about one of my guys. Reynaldo."

"What about him?" Jackson asked. It was obvious that he was growing short on patience as well.

"He was apprenticing with me," Samuels explained. "I had him prepping the pool's surface, getting it as smooth as possible."

"Go on," Brianna urged.

"Well, he's working on it, and then, all of a sudden, the kid starts freaking out."

"Freaking out how?" Brianna pressed.

"Yelling, shaking, you know, freaking out," Samuels emphasized. "I asked him what's wrong and he said he saw eyes looking at him. Watching him work."

"Someone was watching him work?" Jackson repeated, trying to get this straight. "You mean, like inside the hotel?"

"No," Samuels answered, annoyed. "Inside the *pool*," he specified. "The kid swore that he saw someone looking at him from inside the pool."

Brianna looked at Jackson, but it was impossible to read his expression. "Sounds a little far-fetched. What did you do?"

"I figured he had too much to drink at lunch, told him to stop imagining things and get back to work or I'd get someone else to do it. He finished the job," Samuels told them proudly, as if he had accomplished something by causing this to happen.

Brianna waited, but there was nothing more. "And you never said anything about it?" she asked the contractor, stunned.

"To who?" he asked. "To the kid? The less said the better."

"No, to Damien," Jackson answered. "Since he's the one who hired you for the job."

Samuels shook his head. "Didn't want him to know I look the other way when my guys loosen up a little at lunch. Man's entitled to a drink now and then," he added as if he was defending his people. "Anyway, job got finished, we got paid. No harm done. Now I've *really* gotta get back to this," he said, jerking his thumb at the house that was under construction.

"One last thing," Brianna called after him. "Could you point Reynaldo out for us?"

Samuels stopped and turned around but made no effort to walk back. "I could. If he were here," the contractor qualified.

"Do you know where we can find him?" Jackson asked.

Samuels shrugged. "Probably anywhere there's work."

"So he doesn't work for you anymore?" Brianna asked Samuels.

"Nope."

"Do you have his last name? His address? A

phone number where you can reach him?" she asked, getting more and more annoyed at the contractor's indifference.

"I got a number, but he wasn't there the last time I tried. Guy who answered the phone said Reynaldo had moved on. Why are you so interested in Reynaldo?" he demanded. "I've got any one of a number of guys who can work rings around him."

Jackson took over, almost growling out the words. "Because we think he might have seen something he shouldn't have."

The importance of the whole thing clearly escaped the contractor. "Like what?"

Brianna could see that her partner was close to telling the contractor he was an idiot. "Like those eyes he was so spooked about probably belonged to someone buried under the pool."

Samuels's mouth dropped. "You're putting me on," the man cried, completely forgetting about the development he was overseeing.

Brianna decided to treat this all lightly before Jackson called the contractor a living brain donor.

"I'm not that kind of girl, Mr. Samuels," she deadpanned. "And right now, you are going to have to go to your office and get us Reynaldo's last known address and phone number, not to mention his last name and any ID you have on the man."

This time the contractor blanched. "You're not serious."

Brianna turned toward her partner. "Muldare, tell the man how serious I am."

"Like a heart attack," Jackson underscored.

Samuels looked from Brianna to her partner. He gave up trying to argue.

Chapter 16

"'**R**eynaldo Reyes'?" Detective Valri Cavanaugh Brody read the name from the photocopy of the green card Brianna had handed her. The one that Samuels had reluctantly copied for them in his office. Valri raised her eyes to look at the two people standing at her desk. "What, you couldn't find one that said John Smith?"

Brianna was surprised that they had managed to get this much from the contractor. "It's an employment-based green card. You've got a description, a photo and a Social Security number. That's not enough?" she asked Valri.

Valri pressed her lips together and looked over

at the tall, dark and somberly handsome detective standing next to Brianna.

"Your partner's a babe in the woods, Jackson," she told the man. She sighed, propping up the photocopy in front of her monitor. "This green card's probably a fake, but I'll do what I can to locate the guy. Don't expect miracles," she warned. "That's Brenda's department, not mine," Valri told them, referring to the head of the IT division, who also just happened to be the chief of Ds' daughter-in-law.

Brianna feigned a look of surprise. "When did you get to be so cynical?"

"Comes from on-the-job training," Valri quipped. And then, switching subjects, she brightened. "Hey, are you coming to the chief's gathering tomorrow?"

"Wouldn't miss it," Brianna assured the other woman.

Valri's eyes shifted toward Jackson. "How about you?" she asked. Before he could say anything, she added, "I'm sure you're invited. The chief usually does a blitzkrieg when it comes to one of his gatherings, and if memory serves," she said, scrutinizing his face, "I *don't* remember seeing you at any of them."

"Busy," Jackson answered, then said vaguely, "Undercover."

Valri's eyes swept over him, as if to confirm what she was thinking. "Well, you don't look undercover now, so I guess you'll be there." Valri blew out a breath and turned her attention back to the photocopy of Reyes's green card. "In the meantime, I'll see what can be done with this, but like I said, don't get your hopes up."

"We appreciate anything that you can do with that." Brianna waved her hand at the photocopy. "And contrary to what you just said, miracles *are* your department." Smiling, she and Jackson withdrew. "See you tomorrow at the chief's house," she tossed over her shoulder as they left the computer lab and went on to the elevator.

Jackson remained quiet as they rode up to the first floor and even after they had exited the building. Unable to take it anymore, Brianna finally broke the silence with an order.

"*Say* something."

Halting just beyond the double glass doors, Jackson asked, "Is *everyone* in your family pushy?"

She knew he'd say something like that the minute Valri had asked him about coming to the gathering.

"It's a congenital condition," Brianna answered. "And we prefer to refer to it as being compassionate and friendly."

Jackson shook his head. "Pushy *and* delusional," he remarked. "That's one hell of a combination."

Well, she hadn't expected him to just lie down and give in quietly, she reminded herself. "You can call it whatever you want, as long as you come," Brianna said firmly.

"And if I don't want to? Which I don't," he added

with emphasis. He had close to a foot on her. She certainly couldn't bodily throw him into her car and drive off with him if he chose not to come.

Rather than argue with him about whether or not he actually wanted to come, she told him matter-of-factly, "Come anyway." And then her eyes met his as she added, "In the interest of your career."

Well, this had gone downhill fast, Jackson decided. She was threatening him. "That's blackmail," he protested.

"Such an ugly word," Brianna chided. "Don't think of it as blackmail," she told him. "Think of it as trying new things. Going outside your comfort zone."

He had no desire to venture into or outside any comfort zones. Comfort had nothing to do with his job description. "I signed on to catch bad guys, not to party and break bread with the brass."

"No brass," Brianna pointed out, "just people."

"It's at the police chief's house," he stressed. If that wasn't the definition of *brass*, he didn't know what was.

"*Former* police chief," Brianna corrected. "Look, make an effort, put in an appearance," she urged. "If you find you can't put up with it, no one's going to handcuff you to a railing to make you stay. You'll be free to go home. But at least give it a chance."

He shot her a look that was far from promising. "I'll see."

"No, you won't see," Brianna informed him as

if they were discussing something to do with the investigation. "You *will*."

"You planning on carrying me in, fireman-style?" he asked, challenging her.

"Not me," she answered. "But I have brothers and cousins, some of whom are bigger than you. I'll leave the rest to your imagination." She paused, then tried persuasion again. "Since we've been working together, off and on, you've always gone in where angels fear to tread. I've never thought of you as a coward before."

"And that's supposed to get me to come?" he questioned, then jeered, "Telling me that you're *disappointed* in me?"

Brianna looked at him for a long moment, as if she was actually considering his question, and then she answered, "Yeah."

Maybe it was her expression, or just the way she said the word. Or maybe it was just a reaction to the long day they'd put in, traipsing around to different construction sites. But whatever the reason, Jackson started to laugh. Laugh so hard that he had to wait to catch his breath before he could say anything in response. And then, when he finally stopped laughing, he found that he had to stop himself before he took her into his arms and kissed her.

Wouldn't that have surprised her, he thought, his mouth curving again.

"Okay," he told her as they went down the back steps to the rear parking lot. "It's tomorrow, right?"

He knew it was, she thought, but for the sake of resolving this and getting him to come, Brianna answered, "Right."

"I'll turn up," he conceded.

"Great." She greeted his capitulation with enthusiasm. "I'll swing by your place early to pick you up. That way you can acclimate yourself slowly to the—"

"Hold it," Jackson ordered just before he headed over to his car. "Who said anything about you picking me up?"

The expression on her face was the personification of innocence. "I just did."

"No," he said flatly.

"Yeah, I did," she told him, knowing full well that wasn't what Jackson was referring to. "I just heard me say it."

He frowned. "I mean no, you're not picking me up," he informed her.

Still playing the innocent card, Brianna said, "I don't mind."

"But I do," Jackson retorted. He didn't care to be treated like a child who needed to be guided and kept in line.

Brianna smiled as she reasoned with him. "Look, if I pick you up tomorrow, you'll come to the gathering," she pointed out. "If you're left to your own devices, who knows what you'll do?"

He didn't like her second-guessing him—or being one step ahead, for that matter. "Applying to a new police department comes to mind."

She treated it like a bluff, even though part of her knew it very well might not be. "You won't do that. You're too comfortable here."

"If I tell you not to come…you'll still be at my door tomorrow, won't you?"

Rather than answer, Brianna smiled at him. Broadly.

"I don't have a choice in this, do I?" he bit off, exasperated.

"Well, you can *say* no…" she told him, deliberately letting her voice trail off.

Jackson knew exactly what that meant. "But you won't listen."

Brianna suppressed a laugh, trying to get him to come around by using humor. "You're a fast learner."

His eyes narrowed as he glared at her. "If I was a fast learner, I would have worn garlic around my neck the first time I ever laid eyes on you."

She didn't think that was the image he was going for. "That's to ward off vampires."

"And people with a sense of smell," he said coldly. "You do have one of those, don't you?"

Brianna merely smiled at him. She'd worn him down, she thought. At least for tonight.

"I'll see you tomorrow at eleven. We could both use a break from this investigation. And who knows?"

she said. "Maybe if we're not concentrating on the murders, the answers will come to us."

Jackson wasn't moved. She heard him mutter something under his breath, but she knew better than to ask him to repeat it. She firmly believed in quitting while she was ahead.

Because of the intense nature of his work and the hours he put in, Jackson preferred sleeping in on the weekend whenever he could. But because Brianna had *threatened* to be on his doorstep by eleven, he intended to be long gone from his apartment before then.

Things didn't exactly go as planned.

After he left the precinct last night, he'd gone to see his father. Even though he knew that more than half the times he visited his father had no idea who he was, Jackson felt that he should be there just in case this was one of those rare days when his father's mind didn't disappear into a fog.

As it turned out, his efforts had been rewarded. Ethan's eyes lit up when Jackson walked into the small room that had become, essentially, his entire world.

"Jackie!" his father cried, beaming. "You came to see me, boy. Is your brother here with you?" he asked, trying to peer around Jackson's six-foot-two frame.

"He couldn't make it," Jackson told his father. "But he sends his love."

His father nodded, the thick hair that had turned prematurely white years ago falling into his eyes as he accepted the excuse. Ethan pushed his hair back. "As long as he's well and you're well, that's all that counts, Jackie."

Because of the hour, Jackson's visit was short. His father's visit was even shorter. Less than an hour later, the invisible walls of Ethan Muldare's prison had returned.

Still, Jackson had thought as he went home, his father had been himself for a little while, and those brief visits were precious to him.

He was far from rested the next morning. After getting home, Jackson had spent the rest of the evening reviewing all the facts dealing with the Aurora Hotel that he and Brianna had managed to compile so far.

Because of that, it was hard turning off his mind, even when he finally did fall asleep. He wound up dreaming about the case.

Taking no chances, Jackson wanted to be out of his apartment no later than nine. But he fell behind schedule, mainly because he'd woken up a little after eight—still thinking about the case. Not wanting to lose the thread of what had occurred to him while half-asleep, Jackson jotted down a few notes and got caught up in a theory that was knocking around in his brain.

Realizing that it was later than he was happy about, Jackson quickly showered, shaved and threw on his clothes. He could almost *feel* the minutes slipping away, even though it was still relatively early.

Because he didn't want to take a chance getting out even later than it was, Jackson decided to have breakfast at one of the fast-food places in the area.

With that in mind, he grabbed the folder he'd put his notes in and opened the door to make his getaway, confident that he still had plenty of time. After all, Brianna wasn't going to be here until eleven.

Locking his door, he swung around, still moving and ready to hurry off to his car. That was when he made full-body contact with the person on his doorstep, all but slamming into them.

The folder fell out of his hand, papers scattering at his feet. Stunned, it took Jackson half a second to collect himself. It took him less than that to see that the person whose body had all but imprinted itself on his was Brianna.

"What the hell are you doing here?" he demanded, dropping to his knees to pick up the folder and the pages that had escaped from it before the wind decided to play hide-and-seek with them. "You said you'd be here at eleven."

As Brianna dropped down to her knees, helping him pick up the pages, she cheerfully responded, "I lied."

The papers collected, she stood and handed him the ones that she had managed to secure. "But then,

you can't really blame me," she told him. "I knew
you'd try to make an escape." She smiled at him
as she watched him sticking the pages back into
the folder. He made no secret of the fact that he
was angry at her unexpected appearance. "You're
actually leaving later than I thought you would."

About to tell her off, saying that he didn't appreciate her stalking him, Jackson replayed her words
in his head.

Scowling, he asked, "You thought I was going
to leave earlier than now?"

"Yes."

That meant that she had to have been waiting
for him to open his door. Just how stubborn was
this woman?

"How long have you been standing out here?"
he demanded.

"Since eight," she answered simply. "It's not as
bad as you think. I wasn't really standing out here
all that time. I was in my car until about five minutes
ago. I've got a clear view of your door from where I
parked in guest parking. Or rather, double-parked,"
she amended, wanting to be strictly truthful. "I had
to move the car once to let someone leave, presumably for work, from the way he was dressed when he
got into his car." She paused, then added, "I learned
a couple of new words that I'd never heard before."

Jackson looked at her incredulously. "You really
don't ever give up, do you?"

"I don't think I know how," Brianna said honestly. "But in case you're wondering, I did mean what I said yesterday."

Jackson looked at her, surrendering. For now.

"You said so much yesterday," he reminded her, "I really can't keep track of it all. What are you talking about?"

"What I said about the chief's gathering," she told him. "If after you've spent some time there, you find that you've really had enough and just want to go home, we'll go."

She sounded sincere, but he knew better. "Define 'some time.'"

Her grin returned. "Ah, well, 'some time' does mean different things to different people," she replied loftily, then winked.

The sexy wink distracted him for a moment, but he collected himself quickly. "What does it mean to you?" he asked, trying to pin her down even though by now Jackson figured it was a totally futile effort.

Her smile widened just a little. "Why don't we just let the morning and early afternoon play itself out and we'll see?"

The expression on his face told her that he didn't believe a word she was saying. "In other words, unless I walk out of there and keep walking, I'm stuck."

"No," she answered, surprising him because she looked utterly serious now. "All I'm asking is that you give it more than sixty minutes."

He still didn't believe her, but because he didn't

think she'd expect him to just give up so easily, he countered with, "Sixty-five."

"Sixty-five is better," Brianna answered, and then added as they drove off, "but maybe just a wee bit higher."

"Maybe," Jackson grunted, playing along. He'd expected nothing less from the woman.

Chapter 17

Brianna had just made the turn into one of the oldest developments in Aurora when she heard Jackson say, "I had some thoughts about the case."

"So have I," Brianna replied, as if he hadn't been staring out the window, as silent as a tomb, for the last ten minutes.

His tone clearly indicated that he was annoyed. "My point is, shouldn't we be working on that instead of, you know, partying?"

"Batteries need to be recharged, Muldare," she said. "And we do what we do so that we can take these occasional breaks and party. Smile, Jackson. This isn't going to hurt nearly as much as you think."

As they drove through the residential development, passing a park and finally turning onto Andrew Cavanaugh's block, Jackson took in his surroundings. There were cars parked on both sides of the street as far as the eye could see.

He let out a low whistle. "Looks like there are a lot of parties going on today."

"Not exactly," Brianna told him. Finding an open spot right near the corner, she quickly pulled in.

"What are you talking about? There are cars parked all over the place."

Brianna came to a full stop, pulling up the parking brake. "I know."

Jackson suddenly understood what she was saying. He looked at her in disbelief. "Just how many people are coming to this so-called gathering?"

"A lot," she answered cheerfully, getting out of the car. "I don't think that Uncle Andrew ever took a head count."

Jackson left the car, moving in almost slow motion as he tried to come to terms with what she was telling him. It didn't seem possible. "Wouldn't the chief have to know how much food to buy?"

"We all take turns contributing toward these parties—it wouldn't be fair otherwise. And Uncle Andrew has an uncanny ability to figure out just how many people are attending at any one time."

By now, they were at the door. Jackson was surprised that it was unlocked. Brianna pushed the door open with her fingertips, and just like that, a wall of humanity became evident.

Jackson took it all in, slightly awed. "Wow. I've seen smaller crowds in soup kitchens during the holidays."

Brianna laughed. "Surprisingly enough, you're not the first person to say that."

Jackson remained rooted in place. Brianna caught him off guard as she hooked her arm through his and tugged, bringing him across the threshold.

"Now park your attitude and suspend your judgment until you've been here an hour," Brianna instructed. She was serious even though her smile was warm.

"An hour," Jackson repeated, allowing himself to be drawn farther into the house. "And then we'll go?"

"We said a bit longer than sixty-five minutes, remember? You're frowning," she noted, nodding. "You remember." That resolved, she got down to why she had really brought Jackson here. "All right, let me introduce you around."

"You don't have to introduce me," he protested. "I know some of these people from the precinct."

But she was not about to relent. "Some, not all." She tugged him into the living room. "Humor me."

"That's all I've been doing."

"And you've been great," she told him, tongue in cheek.

Before he knew what was happening, Brianna

was bringing him over to the chief of Ds. It was only when he was standing directly in front of the man that Jackson realized that the man she had brought him over to wasn't Brian Cavanaugh—he just bore a striking resemblance to him.

"Uncle Andrew," Brianna said, "I'd like you to meet—"

"Detective Jackson Muldare," the former chief of police said with a broad smile. "Yes. I know." And then the strikingly personable man with the thick mane of silver-gray hair laughed. "Don't look so surprised, Detective," he told Jackson. "Just because I'm not the chief of police anymore doesn't mean I'm out of touch. I've heard all about the case you and your team are working on."

"It's Detective O'Bannon's team, sir," Jackson dutifully pointed out.

Smiling, Andrew looked at Brianna. "A diplomat," he said with an approving nod. "Ease up, Jackson. You don't have to address me as 'sir.' We're not that formal here. You're here to enjoy yourself, like everyone else. And to forget, for a while, all the nasty business going on beyond these walls." About to turn away to go back to the kitchen, Andrew paused and said, "One word of advice, though."

"Uh-oh, here we go." An older, handsome woman with auburn hair and sparkling blue eyes laughed as she came over to join her husband. "You can take the man out of the uniform, but not the uniform out of the man," she told Jackson. "No shoptalk, remember, Andrew? That's your rule." Turning toward Jackson and her niece, the woman smiled at them as she twined her arms through one of Andrew's. "I'm Rose. *Mrs.* Former Chief of Police."

"No shoptalk," Andrew protested. "I was just going to tell them not to allow the Auroras to throw their weight around. They'll try to intimidate you if you let them," Andrew warned, speaking from experience. "You two follow the case to wherever it takes you."

"Speaking of taking people places," Rose said to Brianna, "why don't you take the detective into the backyard? He looks as if he'd welcome a drink right about now." With that, the vivacious woman drew her husband back to the kitchen to attend to his first love—cooking.

"A drink," Jackson repeated. "Smart lady."

Brianna smiled. "She's seen enough first timers here to be able to read the signs." Turning, she directed Jackson toward the rear of the house and the patio just beyond. "Let's get you something to drink and then maybe you'll be more inclined to mingle."

Jackson raised a skeptical eyebrow. "How big a drink are we talking about?"

Brianna laughed. "I'll leave that entirely up to you."

Jackson feigned surprise. "You're taking the training wheels off already?"

For a second, he caught himself being drawn in by the gleam in Brianna's eyes. It almost seemed as if they were smiling at him as she said, "This is going to go well."

Jackson sincerely had his doubts, but he did like the way confidence echoed in her every move.

"Follow me," she said.

He did as he was told.

The house had seemed crowded to him from the moment they'd arrived. Jackson had assumed, when his partner had said that she was looking to acclimate him, that she meant there wouldn't be so many people milling around in the beginning.

Obviously he'd been wrong. It felt as if he'd been thrown in the deep end of the pool right from the start. There was no place to retreat to, no alcove to hide in. Just people everywhere he turned.

Andrew Cavanaugh lived in one of the older developments in Aurora. Consequently, his back-yard was three to four times the size of the ones in newer developments. Certainly a lot bigger than the yard surrounding the homes planned for the Old Aurora Hotel site.

But even with such a huge piece of property, the area was dwarfed by the presence of all the people attending the chief's get-together. Everywhere he looked, Jackson thought, there were people talk-ing, eating and, above all, laughing.

Despite his efforts to the contrary, Jackson found himself being drawn into one conversation after an-other, some overlapping. Some with people he knew by name or by sight. Other conversations were with people who were complete strangers to him at the outset. But not so once the conversations were over.

All in all, Jackson was almost in awe that there were this many people getting along with one another. There were no raised voices, no heated arguments breaking out. No displays of anger at all. In short, none of the things that he had grown up witnessing in his own family.

He half expected someone to come out in the middle of the festivities and yell, "Cut! That's a wrap." But this wasn't some movie set. Hard as it was for Jackson to believe, all this was genuine.

The Cavanaughs and their friends seemed to have a lock on knowing how to get along.

"A bit overwhelming, isn't it?" a deep voice behind Jackson said with an amused laugh. When he turned around, Jackson found the sympathetic smile of a man he vaguely recognized from the precinct.

"First time I came to one of these gatherings— not willingly, mind you," Davis Gilroy added with feeling and a lopsided grin, "all I wanted to do was run. *Fast.* Come to think of it, I probably had the same look in my eyes that you do right now. But it gets easier."

Shifting a drink into his left hand, the detective extended his right to Jackson. "Davis Gilroy," he said. Nodding in the general direction of the patio, he continued, "I'm Moira's husband."

Shaking Davis's hand, Jackson introduced himself as well.

"I know," Davis said, dropping his hand to his side. "You're the detective working on the Old Aurora Hotel murders case."

"One of them," Jackson corrected.

Davis smiled. He was familiar with cautious responses. A couple of years back, this could have been him.

"Right. I know the others on it," Davis responded. "Well, nice meeting you. I'd better find Moira before it gets any more crowded. She's around here somewhere. Oh, by the way, just a word to the wise from a former outsider. These people are the best thing that ever happened to me. And believe me, I really resisted being taken into the fold." He clapped a hand on Jackson's shoulder. "I would have been a lot happier a great deal sooner if I hadn't."

And then Jackson saw the other man nodding and smiling at someone just to his right. Before he could turn to see who it was, Davis told the person, "He doesn't look nearly as overwhelmed as I felt the first time Moira brought me to one of these."

When he heard the laugh in response, Jackson knew who Davis was talking to.

"He's got a good poker face," Brianna said. As Davis left, she turned toward Jackson. "Prepare to have your taste buds feel like they've died and gone to heaven."

He'd been getting more than a whiff of a tantalizing aroma for the last few minutes, reminding him that, in his haste to leave the apartment before Brianna got there, he'd skipped breakfast.

"Are we going in for lunch?" he asked, looking toward the house.

"No," Brianna told him. "Lunch is coming to us. With this many people, Uncle Andrew relies on a buffet to feed the masses. For a while, before everyone started getting married and having kids, he had this really long table specially made so that he could seat everyone together. But then the marriages and babies came, along with another really large branch of the family—"

That seemed a little mind-boggling. "Wait. Where were all those people hiding before that?"

It was a familiar story to her because she was part of the second wave of Cavanaughs to descend on the city, increasing the police department by a third.

"Uncle Andrew's dad had a younger brother whom he lost track of when his parents were divorced. To give his dad, Shamus, a feeling of closure, Uncle Andrew located this younger brother a few years back, or rather, he located the younger brother's offspring." She saw that she'd managed to snare his interest. "Unfortunately, the younger brother had died before Shamus had a chance to reunite with him."

"Damn," Jackson murmured, "I'm sorry I asked."

When he saw the look on Brianna's face, he had to ask, "Why are you grinning like that?"

Her eyes crinkled. He did his best not to notice. "Because you *did* ask."

"So?" he asked gruffly.

"So," she stressed with a satisfied grin, "you, Jackson Muldare, are not nearly as aloof as you're trying to pretend to be."

"I'm not pretending," he insisted, a bit more forcefully than the situation warranted.

"Yeah, yeah." She waved away his protest. "Just come and eat. Uncle Andrew's meals are guaranteed to mellow the surliest of beasts."

"Is that supposed to describe me?" Jackson asked.

Once again hooking her arm through his, Brianna steered her reluctant guest toward a large platter of sliced roast beef.

"You?" she asked, fighting to keep a straight face. "No. You're not surly in the least."

Ignoring the sarcasm, Jackson turned his attention toward what really did look like a feast. There were three kinds of meat and a bevy of side dishes, and that didn't even begin to cover the desserts. All in all, it was overwhelming.

He could recall nights when he and Jimmy had had nothing to eat because their father had used what money there was to buy whiskey. The boy he once was momentarily felt like a kid in a candy store.

"You're the veteran," he said, addressing Brianna. "What's good here?"

There was something almost infectious about the smile on her face as she turned toward him and said, "Everything."

He knew she was talking about the huge buffet that extended over the surface of four very large tables, but that wasn't what he found himself thinking about.

Jackson had no idea where the time went.

They'd arrived at the former chief's house well before eleven, and Jackson had silently promised himself that he was going to find a way to leave by one o'clock at the very latest.

But one o'clock came and went, as did two and three and then the hours after that. Somehow, between the food, the conversation and the company, the hours seemed to melt into one another, and eventually they took the daylight along with it, ushering in dusk, then twilight and, finally, evening.

Jackson was rather astonished to realize that the day was all but gone and he hadn't felt the desire to flee even once after having been introduced to the man responsible for all of this.

When, after many of the couples with children had called it a night and left, Brianna finally turned toward him and asked, "Are you ready to go?" he had to admit that it came as a surprise to him.

"Why? What time is it?" he asked, turning away

from her brothers Luke and Ronan, who were regaling him with stories of what a hellion Brianna had been growing up. He had to admit that he was enjoying himself.

"A lot later than I thought it would be," Brianna told him. Pleased with the way the day had gone, she didn't bother suppressing her grin. She had to ask, "I was right, wasn't I?"

"If you were," Luke spoke up, laughing, "it would be the first time."

"You've got that right," Ronan said, high-fiving his brother.

"Good night, boys," Brianna said deliberately as she took command and steered Jackson toward the front of the house. "Some of us are working an active case," she tossed over her shoulder.

"I thought we weren't supposed to talk shop," Jackson said. "Isn't that some sort of rule at this gathering? As I recall, those were your words initially, weren't they?"

"Well, it's nice to know you pay attention sometimes," she replied, smiling at the man she'd initially been prepared to drag here if she had to.

It was probably the drink he'd had with her mother, a former ambulance driver who had gone on to manage several ambulances, but Jackson caught himself telling Brianna after a significant pause, "Oh, I pay attention, all right."

The problem was, he thought, he was paying too much attention. To her. If he wasn't careful, the woman was going to reduce him to a bowl of mush and that was not the way he saw himself. Definitely not the way he wanted to be.

Chapter 18

"No such thing as making a quick getaway when it comes to your family, is there?" Jackson asked more than half an hour later.

They were just now finally outside Andrew's house. It had taken them all this time to work their way from the center of the house to the front door. There had been a legion of people to say good-bye to.

"How do you keep track of all their names?" he asked incredulously.

"Practice," Brianna answered glibly as she got into her car. "I attend as many of these get-togethers as I'm able to." When he looked at her as if she were crazy, she added, "It's good to feel part of something."

Jackson shrugged noncommittally as he buckled up. "Still think name tags might be helpful."

Pulling away from the curb, Brianna considered his words for a moment. "Well, it was a little rough on all of us when my side of the family first got together with the Cavanaughs who were already living in Aurora. At that point, I would have agreed with you."

"Wait. Back up."

She froze, hitting the brake and looking around. "Did I hit something?"

"No," he said quickly. "I didn't mean that literally. You weren't part of the original group?"

Foot back on the accelerator, Brianna shook her head while she drove out of the development. "Nope. We didn't know anything about Shamus's branch of the family. Why do you look so surprised?"

After spending just a little while with them, he would have been hard-pressed to pick out who was part of the old guard and who belonged to the new wave that had been introduced to that old guard.

"I guess I'm just not used to a family blending so well," he admitted.

She knew he was thinking about his own family. Granted, she hadn't had time to look into his background, partly because she was hoping that he would volunteer the information himself—Del Campo hadn't had any time to come through yet, either—but she had the feeling that there hadn't been much blending or happy moments in Jackson's childhood.

"I think blending is mandatory if you're a Cavanaugh or related to one," she joked. "All kidding aside, you seemed like you had a nice time today."

He didn't want to admit to something that might wind up opening a can of worms for him down the line. "I've had worse."

"Oh, please, don't lay it on so thick," Brianna pleaded melodramatically, placing one wrist against her forehead like a silent movie heroine as she waited for the light to turn green.

Jackson decided to switch the direction of the conversation. "I had a long talk with your mother."

Maeve Cavanaugh O'Bannon was a strong-willed woman who spoke her mind and had always gone after whatever she wanted. Hearing that her mother had cornered Jackson made Brianna cringe.

"Oh, Lord," she groaned, thinking of what she'd overheard when she extricated Jackson from her brothers. "More tales about how much grief I gave her when I was growing up? She exaggerates, you know. So do my brothers."

Jackson laughed quietly. The sound captivated her. "No," he told her, "no tales of grief. Although she did say she was a little disappointed that none of her kids had gone on to become ambulance drivers, but she's proud of all of you. She also mentioned how rough all of you had it when your dad was killed in the line of duty." He turned to look at Brianna. There was no mistaking the respect, or the wistfulness, in his voice. "She's a pretty remarkable woman, your mother."

"I always thought so," Brianna said with sincerity. "I tried to tell her that once, but Mom just said it was no big deal. That she was only doing what every mother was supposed to do, providing for her kids and taking care of them."

"Not every mother," Jackson contradicted quietly. "That's not as common as your mother might think."

Bits and pieces began to come together for Brianna. She felt just awful for what Jackson must have gone through in order to think this way. "I'm sorry. I didn't mean to open up any old wounds."

"You don't have anything to be sorry about," he told her, his voice devoid of emotion as walls that had temporarily slipped down went back into place. "You didn't cause any of the wounds."

She knew that faced with this awkward situation, some people would just change the subject, hoping that the subject would fade away. But she was her mother's daughter and had always forged ahead where angels feared to go. Now was no exception.

"Do you want to talk about it?"

"What makes you think I would want to talk about it?" That was the last thing he wanted to do.

Brianna was catching every light. At this rate, she'd have him at his apartment in a couple more minutes. She really wanted to get this positively resolved before then.

"Well, keeping it all bottled up inside will eventually lead to an explosion, and those usually happen at the worst possible times, not to mention that they're messy. But if you talk about it," she coaxed, "it has less power over you."

Jackson blew out a breath. He didn't want to lose his temper, but he wasn't in the mood to put up with what he viewed as psychobabble.

"Do you have this secret desire to be a psychiatrist?" he demanded, hoping that would be the end of it.

"No, I have a secret desire to see the people I work with happy," she answered.

She had reached Jackson's apartment complex and parked in the closest guest spot she could find. Despite the close proximity to his front door, Jackson just assumed that the woman who obviously thought she knew what was best for him would remain in the vehicle when he got out.

But she didn't.

Brianna got out of the car when he did. This wasn't over. He sighed. He was having trouble tamping down his temper. He was also having trouble with another emotion Brianna had quite inadvertently managed to stoke—which was why he wanted to call it a night.

"You know what'll make me happy?" he asked.

"Does it involve my washing out your mouth with soap after you say it?" she asked archly.

Caught off guard, he stared at her. "What? No." And then, mentally throwing up his hands, he laughed, shaking his head. "I was going to say figuring out who killed those women and how they were sealed into the hotel walls without anyone noticing."

She knew a blatant hint when she heard it. Obligingly, Brianna dropped the subject of his mother. She'd made enough headway for one day, she told herself. She'd got a remote Jackson to come to a family gathering, and surprisingly enough, he hadn't complained all day.

She'd said that the gathering was a much-needed break and now the break was over. "Tell you what. Why don't we go in tomorrow and try looking at the case from another angle? Maybe that'll yield something we missed."

Jackson nodded. Yes, he wanted to solve the case. This one had been eating away at him more than usual. But he was using the case to keep from confronting the very thing that Brianna had told him to.

His eyes washed over her. She looked no different than she usually did. Oh, maybe she was dressed a little more appealingly, but that didn't account for what he was feeling at the moment. A pull he didn't want to acknowledge. Certainly one he didn't want to feel.

Which was why he was surprised when he heard himself asking, "Since you're already out of the car, you want to come in for a nightcap?"

"You don't have any food in the house, but you have alcohol?" It was a rhetorical, amused question. She really wasn't surprised that he had the one but not the other.

"Hey, this is California," he quipped. "We're supposed to be prepared for emergencies."

"Since when does needing a drink qualify as an emergency?" Brianna asked.

The answer came without any thought. "Since I spent the day with you."

They were at his doorstep now, and he had his key in the lock when his quip stopped her short.

"Okay, I can take a hint," Brianna told him, turning away.

He caught her wrist and pulled her back around. He felt as if he was trying to hold on to lightning. "No, you can't."

And then, without any warning to himself, he did something that defied everything he had always viewed as logical.

He kissed her.

Kissed her with a forcefulness that he didn't even know he was capable of. Kissed her with such feeling that it actually unnerved him. Because he had always thought—believed—that he was empty inside. That he *didn't* feel anything.

But he was feeling something now with an intensity that was off the charts. He stunned even himself, and his first thought was to pull away.

Except that he couldn't.

And that split second's hesitation sealed his fate. The very next second, her arms were going around his neck, her body and her mouth cleaving to his.

His heart was pounding like someone who had just found himself going over a waterfall, sealed in a kayak with no way to guide it, no way to even remain upright.

Forcing himself to regain control, Jackson severed the connection between them, his hands braced against her shoulders.

They stood there, trying to recapture the people they'd been just a few seconds ago, unable to know how to begin.

Or if they wanted to.

Finally, Jackson ground out, "I'm sorry."

Brianna searched his face, looking for the truth. "Are you? Sorry?"

Jackson knew he should lie. It was the only way to save himself. To save her. But lies didn't save people. The truth did.

"No," he bit off, pulling her back into his arms, kissing her with the sort of passion that was capable of melting glaciers the size of continents.

Jackson didn't remember grasping the doorknob and opening the door, then getting inside the apartment with her. Didn't remember locking the door behind them or letting go of his last shred of self-control.

The only thing he remembered, the only thing he was aware of, was this pulsating, overpowering need to make love with this woman, because making love with her, possessing her, was the only thing that made any sense in his raw, barren life.

When Brianna had invited Jackson to the family gathering, it was because when she looked at him, when she dealt with him, she saw a wounded man who desperately needed to make a connection with someone. Who needed to believe that there were good people out there as well as the bad ones they were sworn to bring to justice. She was just looking to ease his pain, to erase it, if possible, but at least to ease it.

But when she'd first extended the invitation, not for one moment had she thought that things would escalate to this point—that rather than just spending a day with good, decent people who enjoyed one another's company, he and she would wind up here, in his apartment, systematically pulling off clothes and seeking the warmth and shelter of each other's arms.

No, this hadn't been the plan, but now that it was transpiring, Brianna went with it happily, losing herself in the passions that were unexpectedly being raised and growing to fruition.

She had never lost control like this before. Never

once, not with anything she had ever had to deal with. She just always handled things, doing what she could to make it right.

And she'd never once lost control with a man.

So it seemed rather strange that she should lose control now, giving herself up to the wild, sweeping waves of escalating ecstasy that were taking possession of every fiber of her being.

Nothing mattered except surrendering to his touch, allowing him to explore her, inch by exciting, heaving inch.

With each pass of his hand along her body, he seemed to be memorizing every soft, pliant inch of her, wanting to please her.

Wanting to please himself.

He'd never felt such a rush, never wanted this overwhelming sensation to go on forever. Sex was to experience, perhaps savor, and then move on.

But making love, that was a completely different matter altogether.

The difference between a snowflake and a blanket of pure, newly fallen snow.

Desperate to prolong what was happening because to culminate it meant for it to begin to fade away, Jackson kissed her over and over again. Caressed her over and over again.

Wanted her over and over again.

Brianna struggled to catch her breath, to get her bearings while her head spun like an out-of-control carousel.

While all of this was wondrous beyond belief, she couldn't let herself just be the recipient, even though she was far from passive in her reaction. She wanted Jackson to feel what she was feeling, wanted him to experience the same fire in his belly that he had created in hers.

She was far from inexperienced, but she had honestly never felt this wild craving before, this insatiableness vibrating throughout her body that was silently begging, *More! Please, more!*

Skillfully, he had caused more than one climax to shoot through her. Brianna felt herself coming as close to expiring from exhaustion as she ever had in her life, but she was determined that what was happening was going to culminate in a mutual crescendo. However insane this whole thing was, they were in this together, and she wanted him to realize that even though no words went between them.

Her body desperately wanted to receive his. She might have even pulled on his shoulder to convey her eagerness. But then, with her heart slamming against her rib cage, using up the last of her energy, she felt Jackson lacing his hands through hers.

And then, with a movement that was gentler than she'd expected, she felt Jackson enter her, sealing them together.

The moment he did, he began to move urgently and deliberately, feeding the fire that was threatening to consume them both.

She mimicked his rhythm, going faster and

faster until there was no more hill left to climb, no place else to go. An explosion overtook them, rocking the very foundations of the world they had so recently created.

His arms tightened so hard around her, she couldn't breathe.

The next moment, as air came rushing back into her lungs, she realized that she had just had the most exquisite experience of her life.

He felt Brianna panting against him. Why that would excite him to such a dizzying level, he had no idea. He only knew that it did.

He went on holding her, because he knew that once he released her, everything that he'd just felt would fade away. And he didn't want it to.

Not yet.

Chapter 19

Jackson didn't remember falling asleep.

When he woke up, dawn had only started unfurling its crimson banner through a still mostly darkened world. He sensed before he opened his eyes that he was alone in his bed. The bed where he and Brianna had retreated in the wee hours and, amazingly enough, made love for a second, equally exhausting time.

He'd never experienced anything close to what he'd felt with her.

And now she was gone. And the emptiness that had been filled because of her would come rushing back.

She—

A noise caught Jackson's attention as he struggled to get his bearings. When he looked in the direction of the noise, he was astonished.

"You're here," he heard himself saying, looking at the figure sitting at his desk, sifting through what looked like a stack of papers.

Brianna.

Half-hidden in shadow, she was wearing one of his old, threadbare T-shirts. The worn garment barely came down to the tops of her thighs, emphasis on the word *barely*.

Damn, but he wanted her again. "I thought you'd be gone," he told her.

Brianna looked up at the sound of his voice. Last night had been breathtakingly fabulous. But that was last night and this was now. She wasn't sure just what footing they were on or where they would go from here.

"Thought?" she asked. "Or hoped?"

Jackson didn't answer her. Instead, he grabbed a pair of pants, shrugged into them and crossed over to see what had her attention.

"You're writing," he said in surprise.

Brianna nodded, jotting one more thing down. "I thought if I put down everything about this case, maybe it would fall into place, or maybe something would come to me that would shed light on the whole thing."

Her words were finally sinking in. "You're *working*?" he asked incredulously.

She put her pen down for a moment. "Why do you look so surprised? You're the one who wanted to get back to work on the murders. You even agreed we should get an early start in the morning," she reminded Jackson. "This is morning."

He'd always been all about the job. It was his lifeline, what kept him from sinking into the abyss that his past and his fractured, dysfunctional family had created for him. But suddenly, the job wasn't the all-important center of the universe anymore. There was something else.

There was Brianna.

"Yeah," he responded, "but all that was before."

"Before?" she asked, waiting for him to complete the thought, to go on record about what he was feeling.

But Jackson found himself in a brand-new, shaky world, and the bravado that had held him in good stead dialed itself back. All he was willing to admit was the same word he'd just used.

"Before."

"Oh." Turning away, Brianna went back to jotting her miscellaneous thoughts down on the notepad that was already filled with her writing.

"By the way," Jackson said to her back, in response to the question she'd asked when he'd said he'd thought she was gone, "thought, not hoped."

"Oh," Brianna murmured, her back still to him as a smile spread over her lips.

"So," Jackson continued, as if all of this—

making love with her, waking to find Brianna at his desk writing, nude except for his T-shirt adhering to her body—was all perfectly normal and just business as usual, "come up with anything brilliant?"

As he talked, Jackson absently gathered her hair together, forming a makeshift ponytail at the nape of her neck. The silkiness of her hair felt almost erotic as he sifted it through his fingers.

"Brilliant, no," she confessed, finding that breathing was not quite as easy as it should be for her. "Maybe offbeat."

"Talk to me," Jackson encouraged, doing his best to focus on the subject and not the woman. "Offbeat sounds pretty good right now."

Brianna pressed her lips together, struggling not to allow herself to get distracted by the way Jackson's strong fingers were gliding along the sensitive skin on her neck.

"Sometimes," she said slowly, "if you pull at just the right thread, a whole sweater can come unraveled." She turned to face Jackson. Her heart began doing small backflips. "We just need to find that thread and start pulling."

It took effort not to give in to the rush of desire that washed over him. He forced himself to concentrate on what she was saying. "You got a thread in mind?"

"I came up with the theory," she pointed out, then teased, "I have to do everything?" Taking a breath and becoming more serious, she went on. "I was thinking if we could just tie one of the victims to the Auroras, we'd have something to work with. Leverage, if you will. I can do a lot with leverage."

"So you think it *is* one of the Auroras behind this little hotel of horrors?" Jackson asked, warming to what she was laying out.

"Some way, somehow, yes," she answered.

Jackson did a quick review of the sum of the crimes. "We've got old bodies and bodies that, according to the ME, were murdered in the last year or so." He pointed out the obvious. "Identifying the old ones might present us with a real challenge, but the newer ones—those might be easier to put names to."

He leaned over her shoulder to look at the notes she'd made. Her hair smelled of some sort of floral shampoo. He could feel his gut tightening, stirring. He forced himself to think.

"Why don't we pull up all the missing-persons reports that were filed in California in the last, say, two, three years. Maybe Nevada, too," Jackson suggested.

Brianna nodded. It was coming together, she thought, excitement building within her. They were going to get to the bottom of this, she could *feel* it.

Turning to look up at him, she smiled approvingly at the man who had so recently set her world on fire. "I guess you're not just another pretty face after all."

"Maybe," he said, his voice lowering, "I just need to be inspired." Taking her hand, he raised her up to her feet. "You know," he pointed out, "it's still too early to go in."

"Computers never sleep," Brianna reminded him, although not too forcefully. She was excited about the idea they were postulating but more excited about the man she was working with.

"But, if memory serves, your cousin Valri does. And it *is* Sunday. She might like sleeping in."

"She won't mind if we wake her up. Neither will Kristin—the head ME," she prompted, in case he'd forgotten the medical examiner's name.

His eyes were already making love to her. The very thought was exciting him. "I know who Kristin is. I had a crash course in Cavanaughs yesterday, remember?"

Brianna's look of surprise was only half-feigned. "You were paying attention?"

"I *always* pay attention," he assured her with feeling. "I'm just not always open about it."

"Always?" Brianna repeated with an incredulous laugh. "Try never."

"Hey, it works for me," he told her.

The bottom line had always been to use the tools that were available and that got the desired results. What he did kept the people he was up against off balance, allowing him to do what he needed to do.

Brianna slipped her arms comfortably around

his waist and smiled up at his face. "Can't argue with that," she told him.

"Sure you can," Jackson countered. "You could argue with anybody, anytime." He brushed the hair back from her cheek. "I guess that's what works for *you*." His eyes were all but devouring her. How could a few hours make such a difference in his life, Jackson couldn't help wondering. "So, looks like we've got some time to kill before we can get started. Want some breakfast?" he offered. "There's a twenty-four-hour diner not too far from here, looks like it came straight out of the '70s. My treat."

Brianna shook her head from side to side. "Maybe later."

"What should we do now?" Jackson asked, a hint of amusement rising within him. He could feel himself smiling. She *made* him feel like smiling. It was a really strange feeling to come to grips with.

"Guess."

Brianna was standing so close to him, Jackson could feel the word on his lips as she said it.

His eyes held hers. The feeling just being with her like this created grew exponentially.

"What do I get if I guess right?" he asked, his voice low, seductive.

"Me."

It was really, really hard for her leaving his bed and the haven they recreated. But even during their lovemaking, which was passionate and boundless, there was a feeling of urgency hovering over them, something that made them each feel that they were running out of time. Not for themselves, but for the victims who were no longer able to speak for themselves.

Brianna couldn't really express *why* she felt as if they were up against the clock, but she did. Stopping only long enough to get a change of clothing from her place, they went to the police station. As they drove to the precinct, she reluctantly shared her feelings with Jackson, afraid that he would think she was getting too carried away with this macabre mystery.

"Yeah, I've got the same feeling."

"Really?" she cried. It was more of an expression of joy than an actual question, accompanied by a flood of relief washing through her.

Jackson nodded. "Yeah. Like if we don't put all the pieces together soon, whoever's responsible for this last wave of murder victims is going to get away. Not just with the crimes, but vanish completely. The Aurora family is richer than God. They can pay people off, hide the responsible party's tracks in any number of ways. Those people are rabidly protective when it comes to their family's good name," he stressed. "The public is easily impressed by a famous name, but the public also likes to tear down the very same people they'd previously built up. If our second killer winds up being Damien, the public is going to have a field day."

Brianna laughed, shaking her head. "You really are very cynical. You know that, don't you?"

He didn't even bother to argue. "I know."

"You know the best way to counteract that?" Brianna asked him.

When he glanced at her, he saw that her eyes were filled with laughter. He knew what she was saying and, heaven help him, he didn't feel like balking at the suggestion or seriously resisting it.

Maybe he'd lost his mind last night. And maybe he'd come back around to his old self, given time. But for now, the desire to resist what she was proposing just wasn't there.

Still, Jackson felt he had to put at least *some* restrictions in place.

"In slow doses," he warned Brianna. "So that I wind up with a sugar rush, not experiencing a diabetic coma."

Having grown up in what amounted to a crowd, she'd learned the advantages of compromise early. She could apply the lesson here.

"We did it my way first. Now we can do it your way," she agreed.

As Jackson pulled into the rear parking lot, she quickly scanned the area.

Brianna drew in her breath. "Okay," she told him as he parked. "Brace yourself."

"For what?" Jackson asked, turning off the engine.

Brianna got out of the vehicle. Rather than look at Jackson, she never took her eyes off the woman who was coming toward them.

"For that," Brianna said, indicating a far-from-happy-looking Valri. Because they needed her help, Brianna had called the indispensable computer lab tech before they had left Jackson's apartment.

The look of harassed displeasure on Valri's face did not lessen as she drew closer to them.

"Flattered as I am to be woken up before sunrise on a Sunday and dragged out of bed to come to a place where I spend twice the amount of waking hours I should," Valri said, "couldn't this have waited until Monday?"

"I don't know," Brianna told her cousin in all honesty as she, Jackson and Valri turned to walk into the precinct. "Maybe," she allowed, surprising Jackson. "But I've got this *feeling.*"

Valri rolled her eyes. "God help us, the almighty Cavanaugh gut feeling."

Joining the two women in the empty lobby, Jackson asked, "The what?"

"If you don't know," Valri told him, jabbing at the elevator down button, "it's not too late. Run. Save yourself."

Not paying attention to the advice, Jackson turned toward Brianna. "What's the Cavanaugh gut feeling?" he asked as they all got in the elevator.

Valri pressed the button for the basement and

the door slowly closed. "Something that supersedes common sense and all the rules," she told him.

"And is usually right," Brianna interjected with finality.

Valri frowned. "That's beside the point." The elevator door opened, and she led the way toward the computer lab. "Hear that?" Valri asked, opening the door to the lab. "That's the sound of people *not* working—because it's *Sunday*."

Brianna decided to appeal to her cousin's sense of family. No matter what the price, they were always there for one another.

"Valri, the Aurora family is putting pressure on Uncle Brian and Uncle Sean—and who knows who else—to just drop the case, or barring that, just sweep it under the rug and call it an unsolved cold case. Uncle Brian told me they made it clear that they didn't want an investigation, and if there was one, there'd be consequences."

Valri sighed. "This may still wind up being a cold case," she warned.

"But not until all the other possible open avenues have been explored," Jackson stressed.

"Ah, another county heard from," Valri quipped, turning on her computer. "Okay," she said, shifting her chair and moving it closer to the computer, "because it's for Uncle Brian and Uncle Sean—and the new guy," she added, her eyes sweeping over Jackson, "I'm giving this my best shot. But I'm obligated to warn you, two hours without coffee and I completely run out of steam."

"I'll make a coffee run and bring you back a gallon of coffee if you want," Jackson promised.

"In the meantime," Brianna interjected, "what can we do to help?"

Eyes narrowed, her visibly tired cousin gave her a look. "Other than lose my home phone number?"

"Yes, other than that."

Valri thought a moment, then said, "I'll power up two of the unrestricted computers and send a third of the names on those missing-persons lists I'm going to start pulling up to each of you. You can start reading through them, too. That should cut down the amount of time I have to spend here."

Valri began to bundle the first batch of missing-persons reports to send to Brianna, her fingers flying over the keyboard as names and dates whizzed by on her monitor. "By the way," she said, never looking up, "you owe me. Big-time."

"I'm good for it," Brianna assured the other woman.

"No, you're not," Valri replied. "But this time, you won't be able to wiggle out of it." She glanced toward Jackson. "I have a witness."

Jackson thought it in his best interest to keep his head down.

Chapter 20

"I don't know about you, but my eyes feel like they're totally tread worn," Brianna declared.

Pushing her chair back a little from the computer she'd been using, she leaned back in the seat and moved her head from side to side, trying to work out the kinks in her neck. She'd lost track of time as she, Jackson and Valri pulled up and read through scores of missing-persons reports for the better part of Sunday.

Following Brianna's lead, Jackson shifted his shoulders and stretched.

"Why don't we call it a day?" Jackson suggested, looking at his partner. His body felt as if it had been glued into place. In his estimation, spending a whole day working at a desk was nothing short of punishment.

Valri didn't need any more than that. "I will if you will," she told them, sounding livelier than she had in hours.

Brianna sighed as she assessed the large stack of papers on missing women that had been printed up as a direct result of their search. "I had no idea that there were this many lost people out there."

Jackson glanced over at the pile. There was no other word for it than *daunting.* "You don't mean that literally, do you?"

Brianna raised her eyes to his. She thought of her own life and how lucky she was. "No, I don't."

Jackson saw the look in her eyes and guessed what was going through her mind. That comment about being lost was meant for him as well. He could feel barriers beginning to go up, separating them.

He was an outsider; he always had been. Chances were he always would be.

"Not everyone is lucky enough to be born a Cavanaugh," he said dismissively.

Brianna heard the sarcasm in his voice and she refused to allow it to put her off or to drive a wedge between them.

"All it takes is a positive state of mind and a willingness to join in," she told him.

"Well, if I can get you two to leave the lab, I'm *positive* I can close up shop until tomorrow morning," Valri said, powering down her computer. Looking at Brianna, she nodded at the stack of reports. "I trust those are enough to keep you busy for now."

Brianna was on her feet, picking up the missing-persons reports they'd compiled. There were a great many from the last three years that apparently fit the general description of the dead women found within the hotel walls.

"Probably for the next few days," she said, trying not to let the number overwhelm her. Brianna took a deep breath as if she was girding for the job that lay ahead. "All we need to do is find one," she said, glancing at Jackson. "One missing woman we can link to someone in the Aurora family."

"Sounds more like we're going to be trying to find a needle in a haystack," Jackson commented. He looked at the stack, then at Brianna, and did his best to sound at least somewhat upbeat and up to the task. "All we can do is try."

Brianna tried not to think about how daunting that was going to be. Compiling the missing-persons reports had been the easy part. The hard part was very much still ahead.

She turned toward her cousin. "Thanks for all your help, Valri."

Valri nodded, following Brianna and Jackson out the lab door. Falling back, she locked up. "I hope it turns out to be worth it."

"It will," Brianna said with a conviction she

had to dig deep to bring to the surface. Under her breath, she added, "It has to be."

She had every intention of getting into her own car and going home to read through the reports when Jackson pulled up to his apartment complex. But somehow, given one thing and then another, she never actually made it *into* her own vehicle. For one thing, Jackson invited her in to share the pizza he was ordering.

She was hungry, so she said yes. At least, that was what she'd told herself.

But by the time the pizza actually arrived, food was the last thing on either one of their minds. Jackson broke their steamy embrace just long enough to open his front door and pay the delivery boy.

The pizza was forgotten the moment he closed the door again.

They didn't eat for a long, long time.

"I always liked cold pizza best, anyway," Brianna told Jackson as they sat in his bed.

"Yeah, me too," Jackson agreed, taking a large bite of his slice and savoring it. "Think we're going to get the killer?" he asked after another couple of bites.

Brianna slanted a sidelong glance at him. "Honestly?"

"Yes."

"We have to," she told him flatly. "Given the forensics, whoever killed the first batch of women is probably dead. But this copycat killer or whatever he is, he's still out there," she said with passion, "and if we don't find him and put him away, someone else will die. I feel it in my gut."

"That would be the famous Cavanaugh gut?" Jackson asked drily.

"Yes." Brianna didn't bother to suppress a laugh. "That's what it is."

Finished with his second slice, Jackson moved the pizza box to the nightstand. "Mind if I examine it?" he asked, throwing off the covers. "Just for scientific reasons, of course."

Brianna couldn't help herself. She started to laugh. "I think you've examined everything that there is to examine," she pointed out.

"Just to be sure," he stressed, getting closer to her abdomen. "Strictly in the interest of science."

Brianna lay back in his bed. "Well, as long as it's for science," she said, her voice trailing off.

Her voice vanished completely as he got down to the business at hand.

"These are the reports we managed to find on the missing women who fit the general description of the bodies you've autopsied," Brianna told Kristin the following day.

Standing next to her, Jackson emptied several

folders and placed their contents in a stack on the medical examiner's desk.

"We eliminated as many possible candidates as we could," Jackson added. "We thought that since you did the autopsies and had closer contact with the bodies of the most recent victims, you'd be in a better position to eliminate at least a few of the rest."

Kristin looked at the reports and then picked up the ones on top to glance over. "Are these mine to go through?"

Brianna nodded. "You can hang on to them. We've made copies. Just tell me which ones make it to the semifinals and we'll hunt down the women's dental records if we can. Just so you know," Brianna went on, "a few of the women in that stack have priors, so their DNA or prints might be in the system. A couple for shoplifting, another one was arrested at a protest rally. Two for solicitation," she concluded. "But from all indications, the rest of these women have had no contact with law enforcement. No time in juvie, no priors or arrests."

Kristin nodded. "Okay, we'll work backward," she said. "If any of the five bodies in the morgue resemble someone in this pile, I can have the lab try to track down medical records and see if we can come up with a match to one of our five victims."

"What about social media?" Jackson asked her out of the blue when they left Kristin.

Her brow furrowed as she looked at Jackson. "What about it?"

"Well," he said as they went down the corridor, "I've got no use for it myself, but apparently most people can't seem to make a move without notifying the immediate world what they're up to. Maybe some of the missing women in those reports posted something on their social-media page before they went missing. We might find something to give us insight into their lives and who they hung out with. And maybe, if we're *really* lucky, even a clue as to what happened to them."

Leaving the building, she looked at Jackson, impressed. "Boy, you don't talk much, but when you do, you really have something noteworthy to say. You realize this means a lot more reading for us."

Given half a chance, Jackson preferred being outside, in the field, but when it came to this case, he'd resigned himself to more indoor work.

"As long as it leads to the bastard who did this, it'll be worth it."

"This has got to be the most vapidly vain documented generation to have ever drawn breath," Jackson commented more than a day later, utterly exasperated.

They had been going through a mind-numbing number of social-media pages ever since they'd left the morgue. It seemed like one page just naturally led to another link, which led to another and another. It had been like that for the last thirty-six hours.

"Why would anyone take pictures of their food?" he demanded incredulously, shaking his head. "Why not just eat it?"

Brianna shrugged. "Maybe they wanted to remember what it looked like when it was served."

She felt as if she was reaching the end of her rope, tired of going through pictures as she searched for some hidden trigger in all of these commemorated non-occasions.

"You want to remember a sunset, the look in someone's eyes when they turned toward you at just the right moment. You don't want to remember food," he insisted, his tone bordering on disgust.

"Hey, don't get all worked up. I agree with you," Brianna protested. "But I guess these people think differently. Maybe we could use a break," she suggested, closing her eyes and rubbing the bridge of her nose. All the photographs were beginning to run together and the people in them to look alike. "Say, go out to get something to eat and come back," she proposed.

"Sure," Jackson answered. "I could— Wait—"

She shrugged, willing to put her suggestion on hold. "No problem. I'll wait. I'll just flip to another incredibly boring site."

But Jackson shook his head. She didn't understand. "No, I mean, wait—I think I might have found something."

She didn't bother to suppress the groan that escaped. "Not another page of someone posting someone else's embarrassing photos." They'd already come across several less-than-flattering picures. "I'm still trying to erase the last ones from my mind."

He didn't bother contradicting her supposition. "Come here," Jackson said, beckoning her over to his computer. He didn't take his eyes off the screen, afraid it might just vanish. "Look at this."

Coming around to his desk, she looked over his shoulder at the photo he had frozen on the monitor. "That's a pretty fancy-looking party," Brianna commented. According to the caption, the photograph had been taken at a fund-raiser. Everyone there was wearing clothes that would have set back most people half a year's salary, if not more. "Whose social-media page are you on?"

"I've lost track," Jackson confessed. He hit an arrow that took him back to the last location he had pulled up. "It belongs to Jocelyn Aurora."

Brianna looked at him. "That's Winston's daughter," she recalled. The thin, colorless girl had all but faded into the wall the one time she had met her.

"Yeah, but look here, over in the corner," Jackson directed. "That girl with Damien Aurora. Doesn't that look like one of the girls in the missing-persons report?"

Right now, everyone looked like everyone else to her. "Enhance it," she told him.

"How do I—? Oh."

Impatient, Brianna reached over and did the honors herself. Touching the screen, she spread her fingers out, making the section beneath her fingers grow until it was three times as large.

"You're right," she said, excitement building in her chest. "It *is* one of the girls. It's— Hold on—" Turning away, she quickly riffled through the stack that had been on her desk, spreading the pages out so they covered his desk. "I just saw that face a few minutes ago on her own page."

Brianna shuffled through the pages a second time, more methodically, looking at each face intently.

"There!" she declared, jabbing her finger at the page she had been looking for. "That's her. That's—" She read the name beneath the photograph. "'Mandy Prentice.'"

Brianna held up the page beside the enlarged photo on Jackson's computer monitor. She stared at the two images, one sharp, a graduation photo enshrining a far happier time, and one fuzzy despite the enhancement, clearly a shot taken when Mandy—if it *was* Mandy—was trying to disentangle herself from the grip of the person holding on to her wrist.

Damien Aurora.

"We need to print this picture," Brianna cried. "Hot damn, I think we just got our break!" She threw her arms around Jackson's neck and pressed an elated kiss to his cheek. "There's more where that came from if this turns out to be what we're looking for," she promised, excitement all but pulsating in her voice.

"You two partying?" Del Campo called out, looking up from his computer.

"Just maybe," Brianna told him. "I want you to drop whatever you're doing and get any kind of medical records you can find on a Mandy Prentice. When you find them, bring them over to Kristin Cavanaugh at the morgue. If we're right, the mystery of the Old Aurora Hotel is about to be unraveled."

"Don't get ahead of yourself," Jackson cautioned. "This picture could be just a picture. Winston Aurora and his wife throw these fund-raisers all the time. Just because Damien is there and grabbed that girl's wrist doesn't mean he killed her."

"Maybe not," she agreed reluctantly, "but it's a starting point." She looked back at the picture. Enlarged, Damien's expression was clearly visible. He didn't appear playful or even annoyed. Instead, he seemed as if he was furious with the girl whose wrist he was gripping. "With a little imagination, you can almost *see* him dragging her off.

"But the best part is," Brianna continued, trying her best to control her growing excitement, "if Kristin can make a positive ID that one of the bodies in the morgue *is* Mandy Prentice, then we have a reason to bring Damien Aurora in for questioning, if for no other reason than he might have been one of the last people to see Mandy alive."

Jackson hated being the voice of reason. It wasn't a role that suited him. But he didn't want Brianna being humiliated in front of other people, especially not the Auroras.

"You know his father is going to get him an army of lawyers," Jackson told her. "You won't be able to get near him."

She began to say something in response when she suddenly stopped. Her mind was whirling because something Jackson had just said had triggered a memory, something she remembered coming across.

"Jackson, you're brilliant," she declared. Turning on her heel, she hurried back to her own desk. Typing, she pulled up a file.

"Not that I'm arguing with you about your assessment, but why am I brilliant?" Jackson asked, coming around to stand behind Brianna.

Moving back, she gestured at the monitor. "Because of this."

There, on the screen, was a summary of an arrest dated two years ago. The person arrested was Damien Aurora.

Chapter 21

Dressed in her azure-blue scrubs, Kristin entered the morgue and crossed to Brianna and Jackson. She was carrying a thick folder.

"All right," she said, opening the folder while two of her assistants worked in the background, "I have good news, I have better news and I have somewhat perplexing news." Her eyes swept over the two detectives. "Which do you want first?"

Brianna exchanged looks with Jackson. It was obvious that he was leaving the choice up to her.

"Why don't we pick middle ground and start with the good news?" she suggested.

"All right," Kristin agreed, flipping through the folder. "The good news is that as it turns out, one of the more recent victims found in the hotel debris *is* Mandy Prentice."

"And the better news?" Jackson asked, waiting for a shoe to drop.

"We found traces of Damien Aurora's DNA on Mandy's body. As it turns out, I even managed to lift a partial print from her throat. I think that it's safe to say that Damien Aurora strangled Mandy Prentice—although there are indications that some kind of wire was used as well."

"Could he have used both? The wire *and* manual strangulation?" Jackson asked.

"A bit of overkill," the ME allowed. "No pun intended, but yes, it's possible."

Brianna sighed, relieved. She'd puzzle over the details later. "Two for two," she declared. "We've got him!" And then, because things never went a hundred percent well, she tempered her response. "Or at the very least, a crack in that impenetrable wall so we can finally get in."

Glancing at Jackson, Brianna could tell by his expression that he wasn't about to start celebrating just yet.

"And what's the perplexing news?" Jackson asked.

"There's someone else's DNA on Mandy's body as well," Kristin told them.

Brianna groaned. "It never gets easier, does it? Whose DNA is on her?"

Kristin raised her eyes to look at the detectives. "It's a filial match," Kristin answered.

"Filial match," Jackson repeated. "Two different DNA samples mean that two people killed her. Damien and…?"

"Someone in his family," Kristin concluded. It was all she had at the moment. "In this case it's a *close* filial match."

"So that's what?" Brianna asked. "Father? Mother?" Neither of Damien's parents were likable people, especially not his mother. She could see either person being involved in the dead girl's murder—but why?

"Either-or," Kristin agreed.

"How about a sibling?" Jackson asked.

Brianna looked unconvinced. "The only sibling Damien has is a sister," she reminded her partner. "Jocelyn Aurora is a mouse compared to the barracudas in her family."

"Maybe there's a sibling we don't know about," Jackson speculated.

Brianna looked at him. "What? Somebody chained up in the attic they've never owned up to?" It hardly seemed plausible.

"No stone unturned," Jackson replied. For now, he looked at what they *had* established. "But at least we have the name of a victim and we know someone in the Aurora family is responsible for her death." He looked at Brianna, pleased. "We've got that thread you were talking about."

Brianna's eyes were all but dancing. "We do,

don't we? C'mon. Let's go pay Damien and his family a visit." She paused long enough to hug Kristin. "Great work, Kris! Thank you!"

"It's what I'm here for," she replied, but Brianna had already hurried out of the morgue with Jackson right behind her.

The gaunt-faced man who opened the door in response to the doorbell looked entirely unapproachable. Officially, Tom Howard was Winston Aurora's estate manager, recently hired, it turned out, by the head of security, Rollins.

Howard preferred to think of himself as a majordomo, but everyone who came in contact with the man thought of him as a butler, which was what he would have been called a hundred years ago.

Brianna and Jackson held up their IDs simultaneously for the majordomo's benefit. Lusterless eyes assessed the two detectives and gave every indication that it pained the man standing in the doorway to do so.

"Detectives O'Bannon and Muldare to see Damien Aurora," Brianna told him.

"Mr. Damien is not receiving guests," Howard informed them disdainfully.

"But he *is* in," Brianna deduced from the way the man had worded his response.

"He is not receiving guests," Howard repeated more forcefully.

At that moment, the sound of raised, angry voices shattered the mansion's silence.

"Are you out of your mind? What the hell were you thinking?" Winston Aurora could be heard bellowing, his voice coming from somewhere within the mansion, presumably somewhere closer to the front of the house than farther.

"But Damien *is* receiving a tongue-lashing, from the sound of it," Brianna surmised.

When she took a step toward the doorway, the tall, thin man shifted so that he was blocking her way.

"I'm sorry—you cannot come in," Howard informed her as if he was reciting an unwritten law.

Rather than argue with the man, Brianna turned toward Jackson. "Did you just hear a cry for help? I definitely heard someone crying for help from inside the house."

"That's a cry for help, all right," Jackson agreed flatly.

"Sorry," Brianna informed the human roadblock, moving him forcefully aside with her arm. "It's our duty to answer that cry for help."

Howard turned, furious. "There is *no* cry for help," he insisted.

But they were already inside, and Brianna was hurrying toward the raised voices and cursing coming from the downstairs library. Jackson made sure that the majordomo didn't stop her.

The second they entered the library, the anger

felt almost palpable. Appearing almost frenzied, Winston Aurora was doing most of the yelling, berating his son while his daughter, also in the room, hung back, her face oddly expressionless.

His back to the door, Winston was screaming at his only son, "You have to get out *now*! I'll arrange for the flight out of the country and then I am through covering for you, do you understand? *Through!* It was bad enough when your grandfather was alive, causing mayhem, it turned out, without a single thought to what it was costing the family. What it wound up costing *me*!" Winston cried. "When he died and I realized what he'd done, I thought we were all done for. But it didn't come to light and I was finally done with it! Finally free!

"I won't be put through this again, do you understand?" Winston fairly snarled. "I won't! Once you are out of the country, you are on your own. I never want to see you again! Do I make myself clear?" Winston shouted, his voice almost hoarse. The veins in his neck were standing out so prominently, they appeared ready to burst at any moment.

"Very clear, Mr. Aurora," Brianna said in a distinct voice.

Startled, Winston spun around. He appeared torn between assuming his usual genial persona and being the furious man who found himself standing in the center of hell.

Finding his voice, Winston stiffly choked out, "You're not invited here. Please leave!"

For his part, Damien Aurora looked like a cornered animal searching for an avenue of escape.

"I'm sorry, Mr. Aurora, but I think we're way past polite invitations," Brianna replied. "Detective Muldare, do you want to do the honors?" she asked, nodding toward Damien.

Jackson already had his handcuffs in his hand. "Damien Aurora, you're under arrest for the murder of Mandy Prentice." As he came toward Damien, Jackson began to recite, "You have the right to remain silent—"

Uttering a guttural cry, Damien lunged for his father's oversize mahogany desk and yanked open the side drawer. Before anyone knew what was happening, Damien had grabbed his father's handgun.

Holding the gun in both hands, the younger Aurora moved the muzzle of the weapon back and forth a full ninety degrees. The gun seemed like some sort of deadly windshield wiper going from one side to the other and then back again.

"No, *you* have the right to remain silent," he screamed, an almost crazed look in his eyes. "So shut up! I'm getting out of here and no one's going to stop me, understand?"

"Damien, think of the family," his father ordered sharply.

"Yes, the family." Damien laughed almost hysterically. "The wonderful, saintly family—you mean like Great-Grandfather George, who never met a woman he didn't want to ravage and enshrine in cement?" The younger Aurora was reeking with contempt. "Hell of a family, Dad. I'm an improvement."

"Put the gun down, Damien," Brianna told him in a calm, low voice. "There's no reason for anyone else to die. We can help you."

"Help me?" Damien mocked. "You want to help me?" he asked, growing incensed. "Get the hell out of my way, that's how you can help me," he shouted, motioning them away, his eyes on the doorway and escape.

"Leave him alone!" Jocelyn cried suddenly. As everyone turned to look at her, she moved away from the shelter of the wall she'd been all but pressed up against while her father and brother were shouting at each other. "He didn't do it." The nondescript young woman raised her chin defiantly. "I did."

"Shut up, Joss," Damien ordered. "Don't listen to her. She doesn't know what she's saying."

But like someone in a trance, Jocelyn slowly moved toward her brother, almost transforming right before their eyes.

"I killed them. I killed all five of those tramps. That's what they were," she went on, her voice growing stronger. "All worthless whores, throwing themselves at Damien, trying to trap him with their bodies. He was just too good to see what they were doing, but I saw. I saw it!"

"Stop talking, Joss!" Damien cried. "Stop talking!"

But she just went on as if he hadn't said anything.

"I saw it and put an end to it. Each and every time," she said with a pride that was unsettlingly eerie. The smile curving her mouth was chilling. "It felt good to kill them," she said, almost talking to herself now. "They were a blight, a stain on the earth." And then she looked at her brother. "Why didn't you learn? Why couldn't you stop associating with those awful women and be with me? Love me like I loved you?"

She was barely an inch away from Damien now, and rather than being protective of his sister, his eyes were widening in terror. Somehow, she'd managed to grab the gun from him, and in a blink of an eye, she was now pointing the weapon at him.

"Put that gun down, Joss," he begged. "You don't want to shoot me."

"Oh, but I do," she said with an odd little laugh. "I do. I'm tired of all this, waiting for you to come to your senses. But more than shooting you for being so heartlessly blind, I want to shoot *her*," Jocelyn suddenly declared, pivoting to point the gun at Brianna. "I saw the way you two were looking at each other. You want him, don't you?" she demanded, glaring at Brianna. "Sorry, not this time!"

But Jocelyn never had a chance to execute what she clearly intended to do. Grabbing her from the side, Jackson grappled for the weapon with the woman.

A shot went off, digging into the far wall as he managed to elevate the deranged Jocelyn's arms. A second shot went wild, hitting the ceiling.

There was no telling where the next one would have gone if Jackson hadn't swung a right cross directly to Jocelyn's chin, knocking her unconscious. Damien's criminally deranged, jealous sister crumpled to the floor as Jackson finally pulled the gun out of her hand.

Almost beside himself, Winston cried, "This— this isn't what it looks like, Detective." He was all but gasping for air as he looked down at his daughter, anticipating the depth of the scandal that was to come.

"Oh, we think it's exactly what it looks like," Brianna informed the billionaire.

Sweat was popping up along Winston's high forehead. It was obvious that he was frantically looking for a way to perform damage control. "Look, there's still time to fix this. To make it right," he cried, close to begging. He grabbed Brianna's arm. "If you just—"

Brianna yanked her arm away. She didn't want to hear it. She knew the way the man's mind worked, and she was not about to listen to talk of bribes, monetary or otherwise, tendered in order to bury this scandal as deeply as the bodies of all those poor victims had once been buried.

"I suggest you just stop talking, Mr. Aurora," she told him coldly. "You're only going to make this worse for yourself and your homicidal offspring."

"You won't get any of it to stick!" Winston cried frantically. "None of it! I'll make you sorry you ever crossed me!"

"I wouldn't bet the farm on that," Jackson told him as he put handcuffs on Damien as well as Damien's unconscious sister. "Or whatever it is you'll have left to bet after the board at the Aurora Corporation is finished voting," he added.

Brianna called the precinct for backup, then closed her phone and looked up at Jackson.

"I don't remember ever seeing you smile that widely before," she commented.

Jackson was about to shrug off her observation and say something flippant in response when he took a closer look at her. There was blood on her forehead. And it was alarmingly fresh.

"Hey, you're bleeding," he cried. He examined her left eyebrow, where there was a small trickle of blood. "Did the bullet graze you?" he demanded, framing her head with his hands for a closer look.

"I don't know. I guess it must have," Brianna answered, although in all the excitement, she hadn't felt anything.

"How do you feel?" he asked, taking out a handkerchief and dabbing at the blood on her forehead.

"Honestly?" Her grin couldn't be any wider. "On top of the world."

Winston laughed nastily. "Well, brace yourself,

girlie. It's a long way down from there," the billionaire warned her.

With the sound of approaching sirens growing louder, Brianna offered the man a phony smile. "You ought to know, Mr. Aurora."

"I can buy and sell your family," he shouted into her face. "And I will! And then destroy it!" he vowed, turning almost beet red.

Brianna caught Jackson's arm before he could defend her with a well-deserved swing at the man. In this day and age, doing something like that would cost him more than it would ultimately cost Aurora, and she wasn't about to let that happen, as much as she would love to pummel the man herself.

Summoning inner strength, Brianna appeared utterly unfazed by the patriarch's threat and looked up at the man whose family was essentially responsible for creating the city and developing it.

"Prepare to be very disappointed, Mr. Aurora," she told Winston. "My family doesn't lie down and play dead—*ever.*"

"We'll see about that," Winston retorted as police officers came pouring into the library.

"There'll be nothing to see after I finish telling them about Great-Grandpa, Dad," Damien announced. It was a gleeful threat delivered by a man who felt that he no longer had anything to lose.

"Okay," Jackson declared, turning the people he'd handcuffed over to the police officers. He saw the chief of Ds coming in with the others. The situation was under control, Jackson decided. He turned his attention back to Brianna.

"Time to take you to the hospital," he told her in a no-nonsense voice.

"I'm not going to the hospital," Brianna informed him firmly.

Jackson's eyes narrowed. "The hell you're not. You have a head wound."

"I have a head *scratch*," Brianna argued, "which can easily be dealt with using a Band-Aid."

Jackson gave her a look that said she wasn't going to win. "Too bad you can't be dealt with that easily," he told her. "But I'm learning," he promised. "I'm learning. Now get into the car, O'Bannon, before I carry you into it. We're going to the hospital."

"The hell we are," Brianna said, digging in as they left the mansion.

Brian caught the exchange between his niece and Jackson as they left the premises. He smiled to himself.

"This shows promise," he murmured under his breath, nodding with approval as he watched the pair disappear.

Epilogue

It took nearly a month of intense, diligent work to finally identify all the women who had been entombed in the walls of the Old Aurora Hotel and tie them to George Aurora, or to his granddaughter, Jocelyn.

"Apparently," Brianna told Brian Cavanaugh as she and Jackson sat in the chief of Ds' office, giving him a final summation of what they had uncovered, "there was a diary. George took special delight in documenting the 'clever' way he lured unsuspecting, clueless young women into trusting him. A lot of them came from out of state, would-be starlets wanting to be discovered. He was the 'kindly benefactor,' who was there, offering to help," she said, the words leaving an awful taste in her mouth. "Until he wasn't.

"According to his diary, he felt he'd found a perfect way to satisfy both his lust and his need to 'punish' those young women for tempting him and 'leading him astray.'" She shook her head. "The whole thing sounds like an Edgar Allan Poe book. Kind of like *The Tell-Tale Heart* meets *The Murders in the Rue Morgue*."

"There's a happy image," Jackson commented. "Speaking of happy images," he told the chief. "The look on Winston's face when he found out that his grandfather's diary hadn't been destroyed the way he thought was priceless."

"Almost as priceless as the look on his face when we told him that Damien boasted to us that he'd rescued the diary from the fireplace where Winston had thrown it after setting it on fire. Apparently Aurora the younger used said diary as a primer, a how-to book for homicidal maniacs, if you will."

Brian shook his head as he listened. "And here I thought I'd heard everything. Unbelievable."

As Brianna, Jackson and their team dug through the archives of the family's history, they discovered that George Aurora had been a bricklayer by trade when he had come out to California, the land of promise, all those years ago. At the time, all indications were that he was desperate to shed his roots and reinvent himself, but those same roots had turned out to be handy when he'd started killing women.

The Old Aurora Hotel had been his first step toward building his empire. He took part in building it, working alongside the men he'd hired. And when his lust had finally got the better of him and he began murdering the women he'd used to satisfy his growing appetites, he went back to his old trade. He expanded the hotel, adding not just rooms but bodies in those walls in the process.

"Cement, it turns out," Brianna told the chief of Ds, "is a great way to eliminate the stench of a rotting corpse."

Brian shook his head. "Amazing what you can pick up solving crimes," he commented. Rocking back in his chair as he considered everything that had come to light, he said, "It's going to take the good citizens of Aurora a long time to come back from this."

"Not as long as it'll take the Auroras," Jackson said. "I heard that Winston's wife, Gloria, is moving to England."

"Well, with her husband and son up on charges of aiding and abetting the murders of those five girls either during or after the fact, and her daughter remanded to a psychiatric institution for the criminally insane, apparently all Mrs. Winston Aurora can think of is running away. From everything but the money—what there is of it," Brianna qualified.

Families of the last five girls were coming forward, suing the family for the losses they had suffered. By all indications, the Aurora family's holdings were shrinking daily.

"You did a good job, you two," Brian told them, rising to shake their hands.

"It was a team effort, sir," Brianna responded.

Brian smiled. "You make a good team."

"I have a feeling that he wasn't talking about the homicide investigation just then," Jackson said to Brianna as they left the chief's office.

"Sure he was." And then, after a beat, she looked at Jackson and said, "Why? What do you think he was talking about?"

Jackson's smile enveloped her. "You and me."

"You mean major crimes detective Muldare and homicide detective Brianna O'Bannon?" she asked, wanting to be very clear as to exactly what the man she'd worked beside and slept with for the last month was saying. Jumping to conclusions could lead to a lot of grief and heartache—she knew that for a fact.

"No," Jackson contradicted. "You and me. Bri and Jack." They'd worked their way to that, from stiffly formal to short and personal. And he didn't want to stop there.

"The chief likes to keep things professional," Brianna reminded him.

"He does," Jackson granted as he pressed the button for the elevator. "But as you took great pains to show me, he, like the rest of the Cavanaughs, is first and foremost all about family. I think the chief's onto something."

"About family coming first?" she asked.

She knew damn well what he meant, Jackson thought. "About us being a good team."

"So you're finally willing to admit we work well together."

"Not just work together. We fit together, too," he told her in a low, quiet voice.

The elevator arrived. Getting in, Jackson pressed for their floor, but once the door had closed, he hit the emergency-stop button.

They jolted to a halt.

"What are you doing?" Brianna cried.

"I've got to get this out before I run out of nerve," he told her. Pausing a moment as he collected his courage, Jackson said, "Since we started working together this last time, you've been a hell of a pain in the butt."

"Well, that didn't take much effort," she told him curtly, reaching around Jackson to press the start button. "Glad you could get that out."

He caught her hand, keeping her from doing it. "But you've also brought light into my world and made me feel that I wasn't alone. I've been alone for so long, I didn't realize there *was* another feeling."

"You've got your father and your brother," she reminded him gently.

"They're part of the reason I feel alone," Jackson answered. "Being responsible for people doesn't diminish the feeling of being alone." He took a deep breath. "Look, I know you can do better, but I'm asking you to marry me."

Her eyes meeting his, Brianna answered, "No."

"Oh."

Crushed and struggling not to show it, Jackson pressed the start button and the elevator came back to life for a split second before Brianna hit the stop button again.

"No. I can't do better," she said when he looked at her quizzically. "It's not possible. And, yes, I'll marry you. Right here in this elevator if you want."

Jackson didn't answer her. Instead, he pulled Brianna into his arms and kissed her with all the feeling that had been steadily, powerfully building up within him for all these years.

And he went on kissing her even as an omniscient voice came over the sound system asking, "Elevator No. 7, is everything all right in there?"

Brianna stopped kissing Jackson long enough to answer, "Everything's wonderful," then sealed her lips to Jackson's again, because she had a lot more wonderful to catch up on.

* * * * *

#1991 COLTON P.I. PROTECTOR
The Coltons of Red Ridge • by Regan Black
After Danica Gage is attacked at the K-9 Training Center, she's found by the last man she wants to accept help from: P.I. Shane Colton. He went to prison for a murder he didn't commit, and it's all because of her grandfather. Will they be able to set aside family feuds and grudges to bring a thief to justice?

#1992 THE TEXAS SOLDIER'S SON
Top Secret Deliveries • by Karen Whiddon
When army ranger Kyle Benning returns home one year after being declared dead, he finds his high school sweetheart Nicole Shelton with a three-month-old son—and the widow of another man. Now Nicole has been accused of murder and, despite it all, Kyle isn't willing to abandon her...

#1993 THE FUGITIVE'S SECRET CHILD
Silver Valley P.D. • by Geri Krotow
US marshal Trina Lopez never expected the fugitive she captured to be navy SEAL turned undercover Trail Hiker agent Rob Bristol, who happens to be the father of her son. But the Russian mob is closing in around them and they'll have to survive that before they can even begin to try to become a family.

#1994 SNOWBOUND SECURITY
Wingman Security • by Beverly Long
Laura Collins is desperate to save her niece so they flee to a cabin in the Rocky Mountains. Rico Metez owns that cabin and when a snowstorm hits, he knows he can't just toss the beautiful blonde into the cold. Tucked into the cozy cabin together, they don't know that Laura isn't the only one with a dangerous pursuer...

Get 2 Free Books,

Plus 2 Free Gifts—

just for trying the Reader Service!

HARLEQUIN
ROMANTIC suspense

ROMANTIC suspense

*US marshal Trina Lopez never expected the fugitive she
captured to be navy SEAL turned undercover agent
Rob Bristol, the unwitting father of her son. But the Russian
mob is closing in around them and they'll have to survive
that before they can even begin to try to become a family.*

Read on for a sneak preview of
THE FUGITIVE'S SECRET CHILD,
the next installment in **Geri Krotow's** *breathtaking*
***SILVER VALLEY P.D.** miniseries.*

"You didn't like seeing me with a child?" It could have been
anyone's; how did he know it was hers? He clearly didn't know
the real truth of it. That the baby was his. Theirs.

"The kid wasn't the problem. It was the man you handed it
over to."

"The man I…" She thought about her time assigned to
Commander, Naval Surface Forces Atlantic, a staff in Norfolk,
Virginia. It had been a horrendous juggling act to deal with her
grief while adjusting to life as a new single mom. There had
been only two men who'd been close enough to help her at
the time. Craig, another naval officer who worked on the same
staff, and her brother Nolan, who'd just completed law school
and was working as a lawyer in Virginia Beach.

"Not so smug now, are you?" His sharp words belied the
stricken expression stamped on his face.

"There's nothing to be smug about, you arrogant jerk." She
turned into the parking lot of a suite hotel and drove around to
the back, out of sight of any main roads. As soon as she put the
gearshift into Park, she faced him.

HRSEXP0418

"I was with one of two men during that time. One was my brother, Nolan."

She waited for him to turn, not giving a flying fish how much it hurt him. Because she'd hurt for so long, had finally moved on past her loss, and here he was, telling her he'd seen her and their child but had done nothing to broach the divide?

He turned, and she saw the glimmer of fear in his eyes. Fear? It couldn't be.

"The other man—did you marry him?" His voice was a croak.

"He was, and is, one of my dearest, best friends. As a matter of fact, I was at his wedding this past spring. To his husband. He's gay. I never married, and even if I'd wanted to, that was what, only eighteen, twenty months since you'd died? Scratch that, I mean went missing, right? Because you were alive all along." She shook her head, followed by a single harsh laugh. "You know, a big part of me never believed it, that you were dead. As if I could feel you still alive on the planet. But my brother, my family, they all told me I had to move on. To get past what had happened."

"Did you?"

"Did I what?"

"Move on."

She didn't answer him. Couldn't. Because the man next to her, Rob, wasn't Justin anymore. He was a stranger to her. And she had no idea what a man who hadn't told her he'd survived would do once he discovered he had a son.

Don't miss
THE FUGITIVE'S SECRET CHILD by Geri Krotow,
available May 2018 wherever
Harlequin® Romantic Suspense books and ebooks are sold.

www.Harlequin.com

Need an adrenaline rush from nail-biting tales
(and irresistible males)?

Check out **Harlequin® Intrigue®**
and **Harlequin® Romantic Suspense** books!

New books available every month!

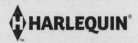